EVEN THOUGH I KNEW THE END

EVEN THOUGH I KNEW THE END

C. L. POLK

A TOM DOHERTY ASSOCIATES BOOK
NEW YORK

EVEN THOUGH I KNEW THE END

Copyright © 2022 by Chelsea Polk

A Tordotcom Book
Published by Tom Doherty Associates
120 Broadway
New York, NY 10271

www.tor.com

Tor® is a registered trademark of Macmillan Publishing Group, LLC.

The Library of Congress Cataloging-in-Publication Data is available upon request.

ISBN 978-1-250-84945-8 (hardcover)
ISBN 978-1-250-84946-5 (ebook)

Our books may be purchased in bulk for promotional, educational, or business use. Please contact your local bookseller or the Macmillan Corporate and Premium Sales Department at 1-800-221-7945, extension 5442, or by email at MacmillanSpecialMarkets@macmillan.com.

First Edition: 2022

Printed in the United States of America

0 9 8 7 6 5 4 3 2 1

To Craig
because they're all our songs, aren't they

ACT I

1

MARLOWE HAD OFFERED me fifty dollars to stand out here in the freezing Chicago cold and do an augury, and like a damn greedy fool, I'd said yes. I'd computed the ideal time for the operation with Marlowe still on the telephone, flipping between my calculations on scratch paper and an ephemeris. I had to shake a leg to make it to the crime scene during the moon's Chaldean hour, the best window for divination with the dead. Fifty dollars is a comfortable sum, and I had foolishly believed I could earn it in time to enjoy my last weekend with Edith.

Naturally, everything was going wrong.

It was Luna's fault. Moonlight sparkled off freshly smashed lightbulbs. It glittered on the wet asphalt underfoot, casting my shadow over the cleanest patch of back alley you ever saw behind a butcher shop. I held up the plumb of a pendulum and tried again.

"Spirit of this departed woman, speak with me."

The plumb did nothing.

That wasn't right. Kelly McIntyre's spirit should still be linked to her deathplace. A mediocre spiritualist can talk to the dead for three days, no matter where they end up, and I was a little better than that. She ought to be batting that silver weight around like a kitten, falling over herself to tell me what happened to her. But the pendulum hung straight down, unnaturally still, as if no one had died in this alley.

Complications. I didn't need complications. I didn't have time for them.

My camera hung around my neck, the bellowed lens stopped at its widest, the shutter tension open and slow. Marlowe would have to settle for scene photos, if it ever got dark enough to take them.

I tilted my head back. Luna flirted around on the edge of a cloud but didn't quite slip coyly behind it. She looked down at me in the alley, not caring that I was freezing to death.

"Come on, little lady," I muttered at the sky. "Give a girl a break, would you?"

I shouldn't even be out here, but Marlowe not only jumped to more than double my usual fee, she promised that I would find it interesting. So far, I hadn't seen anything to merit Marlowe's opinion. More importantly, I had a date in two hours, and I couldn't skulk around this alley much longer. I dropped the pendulum in my breast pocket and stuffed my numbing hands under the armscyes of my coat.

I looked up at the moon again. "I mean it, lady. Scram."

And for a wonder, she did. The silver light dimmed as Luna drifted behind that cloud she'd been flirting with for the last eighteen minutes. Time to step on the juice and get out of here.

Off came my gloves. I cut the little finger of my left hand, hissing as blood welled up. I held out my hand and spoke: "Blood, join with blood and reveal it."

Three drops fell to the cracked asphalt between my feet, landing on the sigil I'd painted there with a solution of radium paint and the spores of a Japanese phosphorescent mushroom picked on a moonless night.

The spell worked by pairing the principles of contagion and sympathy. My blood activated the luminescent properties of the radium and the living glow of the fungus, connecting it to the blood that had been spilled—

You know what? Let's skip the explanation. The ground beneath my feet glowed, spreading from the tiny droplets I had spilled to fill the alley in obscene greenish detail, exactly the color of the hands on a glow-in-the-dark clock, or a—yeah, a fairy mushroom. Blood doesn't un-spill easily. It marks the places it touches. The cops scrubbed really hard, but you can't wash it all away.

I hadn't had a chance to test this spell, but it's not bad work for a gal who wasn't supposed to know anything more dangerous than the computation of Chaldean hours and a smattering of astrology.

The flare of pride at my successful spell design dampened as I saw what the enchantment revealed. The crime scene was straight out of a nightmare. Blood painted the walls—not in obscene, frenzied splashes but in the cruel and deliberate lines of magical sigils. They covered the north and south walls, sprawling onto the asphalt to the east and west, and I comprehended some. But the rest?

They weren't Greek to me; I could read that. These marks reminded me of astrological glyphs, of hermetic seals, but I could read those, too. They looked familiar. But I didn't know them, and I couldn't put my finger on where I had seen them before.

Enough standing around with my jaw unhinged. I had a system for photographing ritual scenes, and I followed it. I snapped a photo, slid the shield over the exposure, and stuck the cartridge in my pocket. North, east, south, west. I captured the sigils and markings in the all-seeing eye of my Graflex. I'd inherited it from my old boss, Clyde, and he'd have something to say about letting the f-stop out all the way and not using a tripod, but I think he would have been secretly impressed with the spell that made it possible.

As I photographed a magic square filled with more of those strange glyphs, the rock in my gut got heavier and heavier. The blood, which I assumed had belonged to Kelly McIntyre, painted the ground and the walls in the complex geometry of a ritual circle unlike anything I'd ever learned as a mystic. This was deep trouble—worse than a haunting, worse than a hex. This was high ritual magic put to the most gruesome purpose I had ever seen.

Marlowe had been right after all. This was one hell of a job, and I didn't have time to take it past this consultation. I wished I could have, even though the whole thing screamed *peril! Danger! Mortal threat!* Awful as it was, it woke my sense of curiosity right up.

Another magazine slid into my camera, and I crouched to get the best frame on the markings along the north wall.

Wait.

Crouching. I backed up and counted bricks, holding my arm up to reckon eyeline.

"Huh."

The White City Vampire could have been the Half-Pint Vampire. The markings put him at about five foot three. How did a pipsqueak that size haul an amazon like Nightingale McIntyre this deep into the alley? I wondered at the state of the songbird's nails. Had she fought back, or was she dead weight? Could I grease somebody at the morgue to find out?

I was falling into the case, and I couldn't do that. All I had time for was getting these pictures. I crouched again, shooting a square of the unknown alphabet on the south wall. The shutter clicked open, and the glow on the walls intensified an instant before it all went dark—or should I say, bright.

"Dammit."

Luna was back from her tryst with cloud cover, shining on me with all her curiosity.

I had another vial of luminous solution. It was enough for another spell, but I would have to wait . . . I looked up at the sky and reckoned. At least another half hour. That would tip me into the hour of Saturn, and that was inauspicious.

Six shots would have to be enough—the seventh was probably ruined. I reloaded the camera with fresh film, and my pockets bulged with 4x5 plates. The glow from the spell was gone, but I gazed through the viewfinder all the same. Something inside me wanted one more shot, and a mystic doesn't ignore her intuition.

Broken glass crunched under a boot sole. A new shadow fell over my path, shaped like square shoulders and a fedora.

"What's your business here?" a man demanded, and then he made a disbelieving noise. "Christ, it's a dame."

Damn it. I'd been pinched, and it was my own fault. I had cast no wards at all. I wasn't great with the invisibility glamour. I hadn't even set up a trip line. I had been sloppy, and I deserved to get caught.

Two men had come around the corner—one tall and broad across the shoulder, the other shorter, standing like a boxer. But were they cops or robbers?

Intuition still had its lips to my ear. I depressed the shutter button with the lens pointed in their direction before I grabbed air and gave a grin. "The scene's clean, but a second look never hurt—Aw, hell."

The flash of an eight-pointed silver star on the shorter man's lapel told me who I was dealing with, and I'd be twice damned if I ever showed my belly to the likes of *them*. I put my hands down. "Evening, gentlemen. Nice night."

The shorter man took the lead, gun in hand. But then I got a look at the bigger one, and even with his figure shrouded in shadow, my heart gave a little leap, because I knew him. The light shifted to shine on half his face and I forgot how to breathe. His chin, his mouth . . . even ten years older and a full foot taller, I knew.

"Ted?" I took a step forward. "Teddy?"

"Helen. You shouldn't be here."

"Helen Brandt?" The shorter one's voice rang with delighted scandal. "You're still alive?"

Ted and I both flinched.

"Shut up, Delaney," my brother said. His voice didn't squeak anymore, evened out to a smooth tenor.

Delaney didn't matter. I was smiling so hard, I could feel the cold on my molars. Ted was here, this week of all weeks. Here, when I thought I'd never see him again. "Teddy. It is you. You transferred out of Ohio? Are you here in Chicago to stay? You've got to be an initiate by now; have you earned your third degree?"

My heart thumped in my chest like it had to carry the whole band playing in my veins. Ted. My little brother, not so little now, standing right there and—his expression was hewn from ice.

"You don't get to ask about me," Teddy said. "You don't get to stand there and ask about my life."

The look on his face tore me open, exposing the hollow spot just under my heart that never felt full. I'd accepted that I would never see him again a long time before, but I never made peace with it. In my heart of hearts, I yearned for one more glimpse and hoped that he would know me anywhere. That he would see me, the sister who he had loved with all his heart, and maybe I'd have something to tuck away in the little space I had emptied for his sake.

It wasn't turning out the way I'd dreamed it. He regarded me with disdain, rejection plain on his face. He saw no one he loved, only the warlock Helen Brandt—and I had never wished to see that in his eyes.

But even as the moment I had dreamed of turned into a nightmare, the gears in my skull kept turning. Teddy wasn't in this alley by chance. They'd been watching the scene all along. Not cops. Not robbers. High magicians, and that was worse.

I lifted the collar of my coat and gathered up my dignity. I was Helen Brandt. He was Initiate Theodore Brandt, and I wouldn't air out our family business in front of a stranger, even if he knew the rumors anyway.

I flicked my hat brim at Delaney. "What brings the Brotherhood of the Compass to such a charming location?"

"Wouldn't you like to know?" he said with a sneer he'd probably copied from the movies. "Who tipped you to the case?"

"As if the White City Vampire wasn't all over the papers?" I asked.

"So, you're just acting as a concerned citizen," Delaney said. "I'm supposed to believe that from a warlock?"

Ted didn't speak. He didn't even move. I kept the words locked up tight, but if he gave an inch, I'd tell him everything. I'd grab on to any thread he threw me and hold it like it would save my life. I opened my hands, palms up. "Ted. I'm just trying to help."

But Ted let his partner do the talking.

"I asked you your business here." Delaney was older than either of us, from the river-delta lines near his eyes, and he carried the easy presumptuousness of long-held authority. But he could gas on all he wanted. Marlowe didn't pay me to snitch on her to the Brotherhood.

I tilted my chin up three more degrees. I had to gaze down my nose to see him, and hid my smug reaction when he bristled. "A hunch. I couldn't sit by if there was something . . . obscure happening. And there must be a pattern in the hour of the murders. This one happened while the sun squared the moon, within a degree of orb to the aspect while in contraparallel—"

"Oh, yeah," the short one said. "You're an *astrologer*."

"Auspex," I corrected. "That's Latin for—"

"Enough, Miss Brandt." Ted talked to me like I was a stranger. As if I hadn't given everything for him, everything I had to give. He stood there with ice in his heart while mine broke cleanly in two. "I comprehend the generosity of your offer, but I am pressured to decline."

"Ted." I had to try one more time. "Teddy-boy. Please believe me. I'm—"

His hand came up, and he slapped his fingertips down on his thumb in a silencing pinch. The words jammed in my throat.

"I know exactly what you think help is," Ted said. "You should leave, warlock, before we take you to the Grand Lodge."

I hauled up my jaw before it could land on my chest. *Warlock*. It hit like a slap. The Brotherhood wasn't kind to people who poked in their business. But didn't I mean anything to him? Didn't he have a heart beating inside his living, breathing body; didn't he feel anything, anything at all?

If only he would shout at me for what I did. If only we could have it out, a great screaming brawl where he could tell me that I shouldn't have done it and I could tell him I'd do it all over again, that I loved him too much to do anything else. But he was a wall of stone, and his partner had a revolver, and leaving was a good idea. A bullet could trip out of that gun, and somebody might get hurt.

I backed up a step, and my tongue shuddered at being set free. "If you need my help—"

Delaney leveled the gun at me, and my mouth went dry.

"Scram."

"Right," I said. "Pleasant evening, gentlemen."

2

I MADE MY way back to State and Washington without a single tear. The cold seeped through my coat to wrap around my heart, and I let it push my self far from the part of me that wanted to sink to my knees and weep my heartbreak over the brother who didn't want anything to do with me, to rage at the irony of my brother coming back to my life three days before I was destined to leave it. The wind froze my eyelashes; I walked as fast as I dared with ice underfoot.

I didn't have time to cry. Ted didn't care one whit whether I shed a tear or not, and if I showed up to my date with my eyes all red and puffy, I'd ruin the evening. I breathed in the cold and wreathed it around my heart. Press on. Cry later. There's work to be done, and not enough time to do it.

I shouldn't have taken that consultation. But what's done is done, and I had fifty dollars to earn. I shut myself in the darkroom and got to work. Eight negatives swam through a tub of developer. I worked in the dark and kept those plates moving, just like Clyde had taught me. The Graflex perched safely on its shelf, thawing out after its time in the cold.

I needed a smoke so badly I was grinding my teeth. But it had to wait until all eight plates were done developing and hanging on the line. Then I needed a blouse that didn't stink of having a gun pointed at me. The minutes ticked in my head, whispering *you're late, you're late.*

I shut the darkroom door behind me, but the markings on the

negatives followed me out of the room. The White City Vampire was using ritual sacrifice to fuel high magic of a kind I didn't recognize—not that I had ever claimed to know it all. Marlowe was interested, but why? Marlowe hired me for jobs suited to a detective and part-time diviner, but she'd never set me on a trail this dark.

And she had never sent me to anything that brushed so close to the affairs of the Brotherhood of the Compass. I did not want to tangle with my former order. Forget the Golden Dawn. Never mind the Eastern Order out west—they're mostly an excuse for orgies, anyway. Forget the naked gasping of witches or the root and bone magic of the conjuring folk. All together, they barely held a sliver of the secrets the Brotherhood hoarded in their lodges, and even a fifty-dollar consultation fee wasn't worth their ire. I'd assumed that Marlowe didn't want to cross their eyeline any more than I did.

I didn't have time for curiosity. I wet a cloth with water from my kettle and washed my armpits. I found a new blouse to wear and dabbed perfume on my wrists and throat. My unopened pack of Chesterfields hid under a pile of mail on my desk. Envelopes slid off the pile and landed on the hardwood, disturbing the dust gathered around the legs. I left the mail where it lay and lit up.

I needed my nerves steady. I had told Marlowe I couldn't take on my usual investigation, that I would do a crime-scene augury, and that was it. And she had agreed to it, and we courteously ignored the fact that she knew well enough that I'd snap at the bait of an occult puzzle. But even if I had the time, the Brotherhood was hovering all over this. I had to step away, and I had to break it to Marlowe right now.

I picked up the telephone, wedging the receiver between my ear and shoulder. I spun the dial six times and waited for the line to click, to ring.

It sounded twice before Marlowe answered. "Hello, darling."

"Hello, Marlowe. Were you expecting me?"

Her voice was a throaty warble, the kind that lingered in your ears. "Helen. Calling so soon?"

"So late," I said. "I managed six photos before I was interrupted. There's a seventh, but I think it's a wash."

The eighth wasn't any of her business, and it was probably junk anyway.

"Six photos? In the dark?" A lighter clicked on Marlowe's end. "One of your brilliant little spells, I imagine."

"That's right."

"I could be generous if you shared that spell with me."

"And lose my trademark? Doll, my weight in rubies wouldn't be enough."

All my secrets were in a book. The book was in a safe. The combination was written on the letter I meant to post on Sunday, telling Edith everything, and maybe she'd forgive me one day.

Marlowe's chuckle blew smoke in my ear. "I could make it happen."

She probably could. I wasn't sure where Marlowe's money came from, but she had plenty of it, and she paid handsomely for my work. But rubies couldn't buy what I needed. Nothing could.

"It's an occult case, all right, but it's too hot. I can't help you."

"Oh, darling. Don't be so defeatist. Give me a chance to change your mind. Bring the photos in the morning—"

"I have a date," I repeated. "I won't have them until dinnertime."

"Bring yourself, then. I adore breakfast meetings. Or we could start tonight, over a drink."

"Sorry, doll. She's waiting for me." And she might not be there if I didn't step on it.

"Lucky creature, whoever she is," Marlowe said. "Breakfast. Nine sharp."

3

IT WAS SO late by then I was sure I'd missed out. I hurried to the Wink on the edge of the Near North Side. I walked into a dim saloon that smelled of spilled beer, and kept on through to the back, as if I were headed for the poker den that ran seven nights a week. But before anyone could spot me, I cut left into an alcove that held a mop closet and another door.

I knocked the right rhythm—not shave and a haircut but close. I stood still as the peephole opened and a light flashed in my eyes. The wall opened, and Sylvia let me onto the landing before a long flight of stairs leading down into the earth.

"Evening, beautiful. You're late."

I shook her hand in greeting, leaving a quarter in her palm. "I should have brought flowers. How's Moira?"

She smiled with pride. "Moira's got her suit on tonight. Playing horn up at WGN."

"Good gig. Tell her *hi, gorgeous,* will you?"

"She'll be here later, and you can tell her yourself." She glanced at the bulge under my left arm. "Check your iron?"

"Will do." I passed under the light of a pendant lamp to creak my way down the stairs and through a damp, creosote-smelling tunnel.

I was late, but Edith was still here. Sylvia would have read me the riot act otherwise. Distant music echoed down the hallway, and I stopped at the coat check to smile at the new girl behind the counter, her hair shiny with brilliantine, her secondhand black-tie outfit just a touch too big. She held out her hands for my coat and hat. She packed up my persuader in a locker without batting an eyelash and gave me a chit. I didn't bother taking off the holster; I feel strange without it.

I turned to meet the gentle press of fingertips on my shoulder, my flight-or-fight kicking up before I put my smile back on. Just the cigarette gal, silly. Who else would it be?

"You need cigarettes, Helen?" Mitzi (though that wasn't really her name) flicked ringed fingers over the tray. I tipped a nickel and kissed her rouged cheek.

"You look gorgeous, doll."

She fluttered her hands and shooed me away. "Go break some other girl's heart, you wicked broad."

I grinned and swept open the beaded curtain to the Wink.

Chicago had loved us once, and the straights had packed into the De Luxe Café and the old Twelve-Thirty Club to come scandalously close to the queer. But the cops cracked down on the pansy clubs in 1935, and these days, Chicago didn't love our kind at all.

Somebody found this place at the end of the Great War and the beginning of the Great Experiment and put a bar in it. After Prohibition and the gallons of blood washing out the gutters of Chicago, this place draped itself in dust and waited for Betty Donahue and her wife, Willie, to discover it themselves. They had established the passwords two Halloweens ago, and we all planned to take its secret to our graves.

The Wink was long and narrow, its chipped brick walls lined with cozy horseshoe booths. Real crystal chandeliers—mismatched, bless every one of them—glittered through a fog of cigarette smoke. They hung down the center of the room, leading the way past the long, well-stocked bar to a round-edged stage, where Miss Francine swayed in a glittering blue gown and sang "I've Got You Under My Skin."

The room was full of women; don't let the double-breasted

suits and slicked-back hair fool you. The Wink was a haven of women, gathered in clumps or cuddled around a special companion, whether they wore starched collar shirts or satin and sequins. The Friday-night women of the Wink could make free, drinking and laughing, eyeing each other the way they'd never dare on the street.

I wound through the standing crowd, headed for my usual place at the end of the bar. A highball sat fizzing next to my empty chair, and beside it sat Edith Jarosky, listening to the songbird up on stage. She'd waited for me. I glanced at my wristwatch. Forty-five minutes, and she'd waited.

She had her pinstripe jacket on, the shoulders sharp-angled and fashionable. Her scarf hung neatly on the back of her chair. She had one last sip of bourbon in her glass; that's how close I cut it. Her neck was bare, the hair lopped off in a tumble of curls so artful I longed to mess it up.

Edith. I stopped just to look at her in profile, at the way she picked up the heavy-bottomed glass and looked in on her last sip, the one she'd lingered over, waiting for me. But I stayed where I was. I wanted this moment to see her, to fill my memories with her, to feel how it ached so sweet and bitter in my chest to see her one more time before I had to button all that up and put on a smile—

She turned her head and looked right at me. Smile. *Smile.* But as I gazed at her and she at me, something fluttered in the shadow of her face. My heart jumped. In my mind, a metal door slammed shut. Smile. Smile.

Edith beckoned to me and I came, helpless as a fish on the hook but glad, so glad to be caught. She put her hand on the polished bar top and I laid mine over hers, twining our fingers together.

I love you, Edith. I love you so much. I thought it until it echoed inside my ears.

"You're late."

"I'm sorry, baby." Forty-five more minutes I could have had with her, if I hadn't been chasing this mess of a job. I didn't need the fifty dollars. I had enough put away. It would keep Edith for a little while.

I wish I had more.

She leaned over and let me taste the bourbon on her lips. "You smell like pictures. You get a job?"

"A consultation."

"Yeah?" Her eyes were bright, excited. "Object or people?"

"It's too hot, baby. I'm turning it down." I tossed bourbon and Coke over my tonsils, leaving an empty glass next to hers. The bourbon sat warm and fuzzy in my middle as I slid off the seat. "Ain't this our song?"

Edith smiled at me through her sand-brown curls. "You say that about all the love songs."

"That's because they're ours. Come on; dance with me."

She let me pull her to the tiny patch of floor in front of the stage. I blew Miss Francine a kiss she caught in her hand without missing a note, and then I folded into Edith's arms.

We'd danced the first night we met, when Edith was still stumbling to lead. But she wanted to dance the next night we met, and every night we spent at the Wink after that. She eased me into an inside turn and I came back to her arms, easy as breathing.

"I have something to tell you." Edith brimmed up with news and it spilled forth in a grin that showed her gums. "There's an opening at KSAN. The station manager called me."

Edith's life was a series of call signs and station identifiers I could hardly keep straight, but I knew that one. "All the way from San Francisco?"

Her smile sparkled brighter than the chandeliers. "Just like we wanted. If I take the job, it'll start in a month."

A month. Oh, but it hurt. I'd wanted to go west years before, but there wasn't enough money. Edith had a good job at WMAQ as a sound engineer—she was the only woman sound engineer in the whole state. And she wouldn't move away to take a lesser job as a switchboard operator or a coffee-fetching typist, and I'd never ask her to. San Francisco was the stuff of dreams, but we stayed in Chicago, where we could afford the rent.

But now the stars aligned. Now she could go.

Edith's smile faltered. She bit her lip and hunched her shoulders. "I thought you'd be happy."

I chucked her chin and kissed it, lips against the dimple that I adored. "Just like we always dreamed, baby. That's great. Do you want the job?"

"Of course I do. But . . . you have some put away, don't you?"

I had five thousand dollars in the safe. "I've been saving for a foggy day."

She licked her lips and went on. "I thought you could work with an insurance firm out there, maybe. Get square and steady."

"We could get a house." I fought to make my smile something she would understand. "Our house on a hill."

It was a lie, but it was a wish, too. A house in the city where people like us carved out home for themselves, a city that didn't mind us much. She was ready for everything we'd talked about in the dark.

She'd get every cent I'd squirreled away in the safe. Every cent. And my grimoire, as sharp-bladed a gift as that was. But if anyone could make good of it, it was Edith.

"You're trying to be happy. For me." The cautious corners of a smile tugged at her mouth, but her worried eyebrows stayed high. "Don't you want to go?"

"There's no place I'd rather be."

We danced through the dream. Our house, steep-roofed and narrow, holding its balance against the slanted street. Our cars tucked side by side, every night asleep in our bed, every morning coffee and orange juice and my turn to burn the sausage.

I held the image of the house in my mind. "It's exactly what we wanted."

Edith looked at me again, words on the tip of her tongue.

I traced my fingers over the tension in her shoulder. We turned in each other's arms, all the universe right there. "You ready to leave Chicago? It's a long way from your family."

She didn't answer for so long I'd gotten my mouth open to take it back. But then she answered, and her soft tone had me on alert.

"Last month, Lila asked her father if she could help Aunt Edith find a husband. Luka just looked at the ceiling. Mother asked me if I'd met any nice men at that job of mine while we were eating Sunday dinner. On Wednesday, Sara dragged me across Saint Stanislaus to meet a man after mass."

I stroked her cheek. "Oh, Edith."

Her expression threatened to shatter into a thousand tears. "They'll never stop, Helen. They're my family. But I can't do it anymore."

She didn't need to say anything more. I would give her this. I would give her the world. Anything she wanted. "Take the job, baby. Take it. This town will weep the day you leave."

She sniffled. Her eyes shone. "We'll go to San Francisco?"

"There's no place I'd rather be."

She danced closer, resting her cheek against mine. "I'll miss this place."

I'll miss it too.

The music stopped. We applauded. Moira stepped up to the front of the stage, the bell of her horn gleaming in the smoky light. She played three long notes before the piano and bass picked up the melody. Miss Francine swayed down the stairs, a gin and tonic in one sapphire-ringed hand. She winked at me before letting her latest belle guide her to the booth where the performers held court, dazzling in paste gems and pot rouge, boiled shirts and brilliantine.

"Helen." Edith stepped backward, tugging on my hand. "Let's get out of here. Take me home."

"You don't want another dance?"

"Put on a record when we get in," she said. "I want to talk."

4

WE WALKED SHOULDER to shoulder along the windy streets, the snow peppering our faces in tiny hard kisses. A couple of women stepped out of an all-night drugstore and picked their way across the frosted street to a bone-colored car. Someone else would wonder why they were at a drugstore in the Loop at this hour, but I knew that place sold dope.

Edith shook her head. "Poor girl."

I glanced at her. "Hm?"

She pointed at the retreating auto. "Her husband's never happy."

Edith had the knack of picking up stray thoughts. She heard snatches of speech like scratchy radio broadcasts. I didn't have the gift, so I couldn't teach her how to tune in and listen for longer than a second.

Ted could have. I locked that thought away as fast as I could. "Does he knock her around?"

"No. She tries to make him happy, and he never is."

"Tough break."

I lifted my hand and stroked my gloved hand down Edith's spine. Somebody else would judge that woman for being too weak to change her life. Not Edith. She had the biggest heart, a tiny bit bruised and full of love. How she wound up with me, I'll never know, but she'd made the last two years one unending song.

"You're getting mushy," Edith said.

"I am. Keeps me warm in this awful wind."

"We're alone now." Edith bumped me with her shoulder. "Why don't you want this case?"

Edith loved hearing all about my puzzles and conundrums. Even the boring tales of legwork, research, and hours of skulking with a camera enchanted her. Sometimes, she'd point out a solution I couldn't quite see in the tangle of facts and speculations that kept refusing to unravel. I admit that I usually skipped over the danger, just to keep her from worrying.

But not this time. She needed to know. "It's the White City Vampire."

Her eyebrows went up. "Archangel Michael protect us."

I squeezed her closer. "Just what the papers call him, baby. Vampires aren't real."

"Well, that's a relief. Why that name, though?"

"Five will get you ten the police have this fact clamped down tight," I said. "They scrubbed the murder scene spotless to hide it, so don't say a word."

Edith drew an X over the bodice of her coat. "Spill."

"The crime scene was painted in blood," I said. "I'm guessing the victim's. The Vampire drew sigils all over the place. Up the walls and everything."

"Blood?" Edith asked. "Sigils? That's black magic?"

"Yeah. It's not like anything I've ever seen. It's—depraved, baby. Anyone who could kill people to gain power is no one I want to tangle with, no matter how tempting a puzzle the scene is."

"A puzzle?" Edith asked. "You're curious."

"Nohow. I'm staying out of it. I took some pictures, and that's the end of it. I think I ruined one when the moon came out."

"Let me see it. Maybe there's something to save. When do you meet your client?"

"She wants a breakfast meeting."

Edith grinned and dug her elbow into my ribs. "She pretty?"

"Gorgeous. Arctic fox and red lipstick, legs up to Heaven."

The wind slapped our faces as we turned onto Washington. Edith hunched her shoulders and stuck her nose in her scarf. "But . . ."

She sighed, and I turned to look at her. "What is it, baby? Spit it out."

"If you don't do it, who's going to catch him? Nobody does what you do."

Edith was right about that. Ordinary people assumed I chased after cheating husbands with this camera of mine, and that's what I used to do, before I took over Clyde's business. An adultery case paid the rent a time or two. But I had a secret clientele who paid handsomely for a Brotherhood-trained mystic. When times got really lean, I used to call around to see who needed a computer to calculate the ideal times for their magical operations. My best clients always seemed to have computing work they didn't have time for, and it kept beans on the stove.

But then Marlowe had come along, and her jobs paid well. And they were interesting. I'd even flown in an airplane once, all on her dime. I never knew what Marlowe did with the objects I found or the people I traced. She never told me a thing. That wasn't unusual, though. Everyone hoarded their power, guarded their knowledge, defended what was theirs from interlopers. The Brotherhood of the Compass—

Shit. Ted was on this case. He'd been watching Nightingale Mac's deathplace, and the Brotherhood wouldn't do that if they didn't have something on the line. And if the Brotherhood was interested, smart little warlocks stayed far away.

But Ted could be in trouble, and I wouldn't be there to protect him.

Edith touched my shoulder. "You're brooding."

"I'm sorry, baby. I'll cheer up once we get inside."

Edith's teeth were chattering by the time I unlocked the front door of the Reliance Building. She leaned on the radiator as the elevator cars raced down to the main floor, ready to whisk us up to floor fourteen. Which isn't really fourteen, but no one speaks about the skip from twelve.

A wrought-iron cage dragged us up to a hallway of dingy Italian marble and grimy mahogany doors, fragrant with the scent of high-quality Darjeeling. Edith produced her key before I did, opening up 1408.

The Reliance Building had seen better days. It was once a leading citizen of the Loop, but its offices had emptied during the Depression and it never regained its glory. I shared this floor with one neighbor and his tea-import business, the reason for the perfumed air. He was hardly around, and never on weekends.

I shut the door behind me and Edith kissed me in the dark.

I dropped my hat where I hoped it would land on a chair and kissed her back, our hands helping each other out of coats and scarves and jackets. We left the lights off and passed through my starlit reception room to the space where I kept my books, and beyond that, to the space where I kept my bed. The bedsprings sang and Edith did too, because she was always a bit like music.

5

I WOKE UP to cold air chilling my nose. It was pale dawn, and Edith glowed softly as she sat beside the open window with a sparrow on her palm, the little bird bravely plucking a sunflower seed from her fingertips. An entire host loitered on the windowsill, pecking at feed and daring the indoors just to get nearer to her, to eat from her gentle hands.

St. Edith of the Sparrows. My hands itched for my Graflex, to try one more time to get a good picture of her. I never had before—there was always a blur over her face, as if she'd moved or changed expression or was about to sneeze. But this morning, I wanted to catch her with the birds who loved her no matter where she went.

The brown-speckled passerine gave an ear-splitting chirrup, and I winced.

She stroked the little bird's head and smiled. "Good morning."

I rubbed at my face and yawned. "Prove it."

Edith shooed the birds back outside where birds belonged. Discarded shells lay scattered around her long, bare feet. She stretched and the fronts of her Bordeaux robe fell open as she yawned.

I lifted the blankets at my side. "Prove it closer."

"You have a breakfast meeting."

"It's not for hours."

"It's in fifty-five minutes."

"And you, running around bare-assed. Haven't you got a sacrament to adore?"

She shook her finger at me. "Go wash your face and get beautiful."

My grumbling was for show. I'd slept like a baby, properly warm on my left side where Edith curled around me like a vine. I forgot all my worries when we held each other.

But it all came back as I put my feet on the cold floor. Edith tossed me my dressing gown, and I snagged my wire bucket of grooming goods on the way down the hall to the bathroom.

Edith was dressed by the time I came back, in a soft green skirt suit with the corner of a lace veil peeking out of her pocket.

"I can help you with that bad photo when I get back," Edith said.

"That'd be swell. I'll have everything set up for you."

She stole a kiss and my cigarettes before heading out to pray before the body of Christ.

Just before I left the office, I slipped inside my darkroom and took down the negative I'd shot from the hip, the one of Ted and his irritating partner. Edith didn't need to know that my brother was in town. It was easier if I just didn't mention it. I slipped the plate into an envelope and ducked out, running late to meet Marlowe.

Dozens of feet had pounded a path up State Street for the white sale at Marshall Field's. North Side bargain hunters filled the booths at Joe's Café, and I stopped in at the drugstore for more Chesterfields. The clerk looked twice, but he let me have them, assuming they were for an absent husband. Two packs, since Edith would steal half of mine and even the drugstore closed down on Sunday. I slipped them in my purse while waiting at the corner for the light to change.

State Street. I would miss it. I'd miss chess with my neighbor Kamal, miss the special at Joe's, miss growling at the *Tribune*, and God, would I miss Edith.

I squared my shoulders and marched into the Palmer House hotel, where Marlowe lived.

I'd been here a hundred times before—well. Ninety-one. The lobby soared overhead, all broad columns and curved vaults. I walked past the trunks of tall floor lamps branched with clustered electric torches, leaving the ceiling clear for the medallions painted there. I winked at Venus for luck, playing it cool as I sauntered across the mirror-shiny floor.

"Miss Brandt." Antoine, the day concierge, stood sentry before the elevator that rose to the top, but he smiled wide at my arrival. "Marlowe is expecting you directly. What a smart-looking coat."

"Same coat as always," I said, breezy and charming. "How is Marlowe this morning?"

"Satisfied," he said. "I suspect that's your doing."

I let my lips curve and did nothing to disturb his assumptions about why I was permitted upstairs. "Lovely to see you, Antoine. Amos!"

I turned my attention to the smiling black man who worked the elevator that ran exclusively to the penthouse. "Good morning, Miss Brandt."

I had the coin in my hand before I put my toes on the inlaid marble line that marked the border between the ordinary domain of the Palmer House and Marlowe's elevator. I held up my palm, and Liberty, caught in mid-stride on a half-dollar, shone softly in its hollow.

Amos nodded. It was coin silver, but it paid my fare.

He pressed buttons on the control panel in a secret pattern, and the warm, magnetic feel of the lift chamber's multilayered wards softened. I stepped inside, careful to place my feet into the protective circle in the center of the floor.

The wards came back with enough force to make the hair on my arms prickle, and we rose to the top. Amos put out his white-gloved hand and I took it, allowing him to escort me across the elevator threshold, past the trap that would spring if I crossed it without him. He slipped the coin into his pocket and left me with Julian. My shoe rubbers settled on a mat before I sullied the luxurious sprawl of white carpet. Julian took my hat and coat, left me my iron, and led me deeper into Marlowe's domain, guided by the sounds of a Gershwin tune.

It led to the vast, white-carpeted room scattered with dove-gray sofas, lush parlor palms, and a full view of Lake Michigan, a bulwark of jagged ice riming its shore. This view was a million bucks if it was a dime, and from up here, you could see straight into the morning's eyes.

Another servant tickled the ivories, and Marlowe strode into the plush room on blue-ribbon legs. They flashed through the opening of a snowy white dressing gown, the marabou tufts on her slippers fluttering over red-painted toes to match the red on her slim hands, the red on her painted mouth.

God, what a dish. Curving and flawlessly golden, with her platinum hair out of a bottle and dark gull's-wing brows to match the nighttime depths of her eyes, every swaying inch of her an invitation. A thousand ships would have been honored to sail for her.

I couldn't imagine a sparrow lighting on her fingers.

"Helen." She took both my hands in hers, tilting her face for a kiss near my left cheek. She branded me with scarlet lips.

"Marlowe. Thank you for inviting me to breakfast."

"The pleasure's all mine. Shall we do business?"

I tucked her hand in the crook of my elbow and took her to the breakfast table. Julian wheeled up a trolley of covered dishes, champagne in a bucket, and a pot of coffee smelling like seduction. I pulled out her chair and then seated myself, trying not to drool over a cup that would make me mourn every burnt drop I ever tossed over my tongue at Joe's.

Marlowe spread a napkin over her lap and nodded. Julian whisked the polished silver domes away, presenting breakfast.

"Eggs Benedict and Dom Pérignon? Doll, you're spoiling me."

A sheaf of silver-screen hair swung back from her cheek as she smiled. "It's a 1929."

"Hell of a year."

"Indeed. You were still a Mystic of the Compass, were you not?"

"I don't believe I've ever tasted a '29. Are we celebrating?"

"I thought you might appreciate it," she answered. "What can you tell me about the scene?"

"Over breakfast?"

She cut a slice of her egg. "I can take it. Try your coffee first."

I took my first sip and God stroked my hair. It was smooth, the unsweet hint of fruit and flowers unfolding as I swallowed. When I opened my eyes, Marlowe was watching me like she saw something good to eat.

"I adore watching a beautiful woman in pleasure."

"Don't blink, doll; I'm having another sip." But I held back some and she knew it, spearing a slice of California orange on her silver fork with a little pout.

"Go on. If you won't play, talk."

"It's ritual murder. Like nothing I've ever seen. There were glyphs I didn't recognize painted in Kelly McIntyre's blood on the ground and on the walls."

"What were they for?"

"I don't know."

"Speculate," she ordered.

"The sacrifice was part of the ritual. The energy of her death was required," I said, and the thought snaked cold revulsion up my spine. "But it was a two-parter. The operator used her blood to mark, charge, and cast the spell."

Marlowe took a long, considering sip of her champagne. "What kind of spell?"

I shook my head. "No idea. I'll gather what I can from the prints."

"But what's your hypothesis, based on what you saw?"

"I never did an augury. Her spirit was already gone," I said. "And the pictures are all I'll do. You need another gumshoe."

"Impossible," Marlowe said. "There's no one else like you."

"Puts a crimp in your plans, I guess. But the Brotherhood of the Compass is pissing circles around that scene. I'm not at my most charming when someone points a gun at me."

"I can provide incentive." She leaned over her plate. "A thousand dollars, cash."

A thousand—listen, I like money. I do. A thousand dollars gave me pause. But I couldn't take Marlowe's money for this one. It wouldn't be honorable. "I'm sorry. I can't do it."

"All right, then." She cocked a smoky black eyebrow at me and smiled as her eyes changed from night-burnished brown to glowing, unnatural red; red as Hell's blazes. "A thousand dollars, cash . . . and your soul."

The music faded. My breath halted, not wanting to disturb the silence while I rewound the reel twenty seconds to make sure I had heard what I thought I'd heard.

A thousand dollars, cash . . . and my soul.

I swallowed my coffee very carefully.

Once upon a time, I crawled out of the ruin of an overturned car and didn't stop until I lay gasping on my back in the middle of an icy Ohio crossroads. Huge flakes of snow hit my face as I called out to the devil, desperate to bring my family back, desperate enough to give anything.

I called to the devil, and the devil came to me.

But almost as soon as I had it, I lost it all again. Ted told the Brotherhood what I'd done. They cast me out, left me to scrape and conjure on my own. They didn't have a choice, even if I was the best mystic this side of the Mississippi. I had done the worst thing anyone could imagine. Soul-bargaining was the only likely act in the whole Anathemata—who had ever seen a unicorn or an angel, much less killed one?

I suffered through slinging hash and the boss pinching my ass for almost a year before I took a want ad to the Reliance Building. I went to work for a man who taught me how to snoop, pick locks, and hunt down the truth. When Clyde died, I kept paying the rent on the office, and no one seemed to mind.

But every day, I woke up knowing that January 13, 1941, was my last day on Earth. I lived ten years waiting for that handsome devil who gave me exactly what I deserved. But here was this doll-faced femme, my best client, smiling as she told me it was Christmas all over again.

A demon. I should have known before now. I should have figured it out. What kind of a detective was I?

Marlowe waited patiently while I picked myself up off the floor. She didn't even smirk knowingly as I unfroze and tried to play it smooth, leaning back and sipping coffee like my guts hadn't turned to water. "You hold my IOU?"

"It wasn't hard to get," she replied. "So. Do you want your soul back or not?"

I took a bite of my eggs like I was thinking about it. "And all I have to do for my soul and a thousand dollars is find the White City Vampire."

She lifted her half-filled coupe of champagne. "Correct."

"That's quite the offer," I mused. "Plus expenses?"

Marlowe threw back her head and laughed. "You're all right, Helen Brandt. It's a deal."

"Not so fast," I said. "I have conditions."

ACT II

1

MY TERMS WERE simple: I don't do confrontations. I'd find the White City Vampire, but after that, it was Marlowe's mess. I would contact her as soon as I discovered his identity and location, and I would get the other half of the money and the payment that really mattered.

My soul. My *soul.* The words thumped along with the rhythm of my steps and the excited throb of my heart. We would go out west together, Edith and I. We could live a real life together. We could get old. I had never let myself dream about this.

But now I could reach out and treasure what everyone took for granted—a future. A future with Edith, and I was going to blubber right there on the street if I let myself feel what pulsed deep in the hollow of my throat. I put my head down and smiled, hugging myself. My soul. My *soul. And* a thousand dollars, plus expenses.

Five hundred clams bulging in my purse made me want to run up to the Reliance Building and put it in the safe. Instead, I swung my arms and strolled back to State and Washington, bypassing my office on the corner to join the throng of shoppers streaming into Marshall Field's for the white sale. I didn't gawk at the crystal or linger over the displays, neatly avoiding the genteel hatred seething from the women fighting for matching sheets and towels.

I rode the escalator up to Men's Fashions on the third floor, which was no more peaceful. Wives aplenty rifled through crisp white shirts, reading the tags for collar and sleeve length. A discreet sign noted the prices, and I just about dug into a display myself—I like a shirt and tie from time to time, and Edith was a knockout in a suit. But tradition ruled my actions. There were rules, and the first was that I could only buy what I needed for the upcoming operation.

"May I help you?"

The clerk was as handsome as an Arrow Collar man, and he smiled back when I fluttered at him. "I'm looking for a box of silk handkerchiefs."

He halted on the way to the sale bins. "Silk? Satin or twill?"

"Satin, please."

He changed his reflexive moue to thinned lips. "We have none on discount. I hope that's all right."

"That's fine." Another rule of gathering spell components—pay a fair price.

His smile came back, and really, he was wasted as a shop clerk, with a chin like that. "This way, please."

A few minutes later, I walked out of Marshall Field's with my box of silk hankies and a receipt for Marlowe. I turned away from the Reliance Building and went north, moving past the theaters to walk into the steamy warmth of the Sunrise Café, which served better hash than Joe's but closed at three o'clock.

I sat down at the long bar, paid my seat's rent with an order of coffee, and checked for a copy of the paper. They only had the *Tribune*, but I took it without grimacing too much. The Trib was wrong about the New Deal, and they were wrong about the War Aid Bill, and they'll be wrong again next week too, but at least I didn't have to put down two cents to read it.

Senators to Fight F. D. R. Bill, rang the headline. *Demand for Unlimited Power Over Arms Stuns Congress.* Oh, boy. I skipped it for my health and went to the obituaries.

I found what I was looking for right under a picture of Kelly herself. It lamented her death, just shy of her twenty-sixth birthday, tragically taken before her time. She had risen from obscure poverty when an executive from NBC heard her singing while washing dishes in a diner almost ten years before.

Ten years. I got my scratch pad out of my purse and tried to keep the cash from popping into view as I dug around for my pen. *Kelly McIntyre,* I wrote neatly across the top of the page. *Lucky break sometime in 1930–1931.*

When? Narrowing that time frame down meant an afternoon in the newspaper morgue I didn't have time for, but I had to start somewhere.

I coated my tongue with a black brew that wasn't even a third cousin to the ambrosia I'd sipped at Marlowe's table. The waitress flicked a glance as I scratched out my notes, paging through the paper to scan the headlines.

There it is. *Police Stymied by White City Vampire; No New Leads in Case.* I scanned it, but like the headline said, the story was just churning the case to keep it in the papers. After noting the names of the White City Vampire's other victims, I reckoned some dates and put down two bits for the coffee, plus a tip.

The Trib was wrong about politics, but they carried more obituaries than anyone else. I lifted my collar against the wind and aimed for the gothic, sloping shoulders of the Tribune Tower.

2

AN HOUR IN the newspaper morgue netted me the sad story of the White City Vampire's first victim—Curtis Johnson, haberdasher, whose line of silk neckties had become a craze among the fashionable set ten years earlier. Before they caught fire, he'd been stretching to pay his rent. Lawrence Hale had been a plumber's apprentice before he published *Thrifty Home Digest,* a ladies' magazine that gave pantry-stretching recipe tips and compelling, confessional serials that ended on irresistible cliffhangers. He'd made so much money, he'd bought a house in South Shore for him and his lifelong friend, Lewis Chapman. Adelaide Lamont had been Adelaide Swift until she'd suddenly married Tyrone Lamont, a handsome actor who voiced *Get Dick Smith* on WGN. She'd been his seamstress before they'd eloped. She died October sixth, just a few weeks shy of her tenth wedding anniversary, just in case I needed a mallet to drive the point home.

Damn it all! I'd been boondoggled. Greedy, curious fool. I had to count to a hundred in German inside my head to keep from swearing out loud in the archive. Shame, shame on me for trusting a demon. I should have known there was a hook in her bait.

When someone makes a deal with a devil, they usually get ten years to enjoy it. Was it worth the paper castle on the lake? Was it worth selling fashionable ties? Was it worth a man who didn't notice you until you'd given up your soul?

It must have been. I couldn't judge their choices. Not when I'd made mine. But Marlowe knew damn well what this pattern meant. She'd played me like a lute, and shame on me for not stopping to ask questions before I leapt on the chance to get my soul back.

I took my notes on the victims and their murder sites, and let the wind shove me around as I marched back into the Loop and headed toward Lake Michigan.

3

A GOOD HOTEL concierge can smell trouble the moment the front doors open, and I surely reeked of it by the time I stalked into the jewel-cut lobby of Palmer House. Antoine's head came up as my heels clicked on the shiny stone tiles, and his nostrils flared. At his gesture, a couple of broad-shouldered bellhops fell in and blocked the way to the elevator. Antoine wove out from behind the front counter, polite but unsmiling.

"How may we assist you?"

I tugged on the sleeves of my coat, settling their rumples. "I need to see Marlowe."

"You are not listed as one of her appointments, Madame." That wasn't the buttery, smiling tone he'd used when I'd strolled up this morning for eggs benny and champagne. I was on thin ice if I didn't fly right—

I glanced at my watch. It was still the hour of Venus for another three minutes. Time to break a leg. Her image was painted on the ceiling just over my head, and I drew her power down and wrapped it around my shoulders like a stole. I shot one hip out, sloping my shoulders the other way.

"Oh, I know I'm not." I tinkled out a little laugh, palms open and on display. "But you know how I was here this morning? Well, silly little me forgot something . . . personal in her suite. I really need it back right away. If I could just call up—or I could write a note, if she's not taking calls? Julian would know better than I would."

I delivered that last line with a titter and the tiniest mental push. I wasn't good at charm spells, but I had enough mojo for this. The concierge nodded, his expression softening.

"I could send a note up, if you like."

"Oh, you're a dear. Just a dear," I gushed.

I had caught glimpses of some of Marlowe's ladies over the years. She liked them beautiful, or unique, and I guess I was close enough to her taste for Antoine to believe it. He brought me stationery and an envelope, and I did my best to pout out my lip as I put my Waterman to paper and wrote:

> *Marlowe;*
> *We need to talk, darling. There's one little thing you*
> *forgot to mention when we made our agreement.*
> *Take your time. I'll wait.*
>
> *Helen*

I took out a vial of Evening in Paris from my handbag, pushing the sheaf of bills aside, and dabbed a little heart on the page. Antoine accepted the perfumed envelope and took me to a plush seat in the lobby before he delivered the missive into Amos's hands.

I settled into deep red velvet, tufted and spring-padded, and while I waited, I murmured holy psalms under my breath, casting every syllable straight up to the twenty-fifth floor. I made it to *"Thy statutes have been my songs in the house of my pilgrimage"* before the elevator doors opened and Amos beckoned for me.

I kept silent as the elevator whisked us to the top, and I squeezed his gloved hand before I set my feet on the snowy white carpet for the second time that day. Julian led me past the long concert piano and the tall windows, past the parlor where we usually drank cold-hearted gin. He took me down a long hall, deeper into Marlowe's territory than I'd ever gone. I smelled roses and warm water as the door opened and Julian ushered me into a bathing chamber fit for a Roman emperor.

The air caressed warm and humid on my cheeks. Soft splashing led me to a huge square tub—no. It was too big to be called a tub, even filled to overflowing with bubbles. Vases of fresh-cut, full-blooming red roses surrounded her bath, their perfume so thick I could taste it. In the middle of a sea of suds lounged Marlowe, her carefully arched eyebrows knit together in irritation.

"I hate that particular psalm," she said.

I shrugged. "I imagine you hate them all."

She pouted at me and plucked up a half-full coupe of champagne. Rose-scented bubbles parted to reveal pink-tinted water. "Well, go on and spit it out. What's got your hair in a knot?"

"You screwed me," I said, and I kept going even though Marlowe's eyes rolled in a way that said, *Really, darling, what did you expect?* "The White City Vampire's victims were all demon-claimed. It's a turf war, isn't it? You dropped me into the middle of your turf war."

Marlowe blinked her pretty eyes at me. "You figured that out fast. Yes. Nightingale McIntyre's soul was mine. I don't appreciate having it stolen."

"Then give me a lead, at least," I said. "Whose soul is next on the dock?"

Marlowe sipped her bubbly. "Darling, you're quicker than that. It's you."

I had to stop for a moment. Honestly, what was wrong with me? I knew the answer: Hope was what ailed me, and I had stretched out my hand so fast, I hadn't thought of anything else. Marlowe had offered the one thing that was worth risking everything for. I couldn't have walked away from this. She knew it, and I knew it. But Marlowe could have at least done the good deed of warning me.

But everything is negotiable. Marlowe needed me. I'd already squeezed her for expenses. Why not more? "So, you can't drag me downstairs on my due date. Who's going to find your competition if I'm not up here losing shoe leather?"

"Consider it an incentive." Marlowe lifted one leg from the water. Soap bubbles scudded down her thigh as she twisted the hot-water tap open with her red-painted toes. "Now that you know the Vampire's victims are soulless, you're that much closer to catching him."

"Because he'll be coming after me."

"Prettiest bait I ever saw." Marlowe lifted her glass in salute. "Clears the mind, doesn't it? Makes you focus on what's really important."

"I can't tangle with a demon."

"Darling, I never asked you to." She pulled a long, slender cigarette from a crystal bowl and popped it between her lips. The end ignited without so much as a twitch of her eyebrow, and she smiled at me through a veil of smoke. "You find the White City Vampire—or he finds you. Then you call me, and I'll come running, I promise you."

"You *promise*?" I asked, the outrage making my voice break. "Pinky swear and everything? How can I trust you'll come?"

Her smile disappeared. My throat squeezed shut. The edges of my vision blackened. I tried to suck down a breath, and a bolt of hot anguish struck my chest.

"Don't question my word, Elena Brandt." Marlowe said softly. "I don't like it."

She let me struggle for a ten count before she let me go. My knees hit pearly white marble with a bruising thud. Air whistled down my throat and filled my shuddering lungs. I gulped down another breath, clutched my pounding chest, and thrust a pin into the sob that fluttered at the back of my throat. Damned if I'd let it free.

"Noted," I choked out. "Thanks for the clarification."

"Don't come back here without an appointment." She drank the last swallow of champagne, but from her expression, there was no pleasure in it. "Julian will see you out."

4

DEMONS. GOD DAMN. I'd gotten exactly the trouble I deserved. Greedy. Shortsighted. Gullible. Curious. I berated myself all the way back along Washington Street, still muttering as I rode the heavily warded elevator up to my office.

I dialed the safe open before I took my coat off, stashing the money on the shelf that held the rest of it, and I pulled a wooden box off the lower shelf to take back to my desk.

Demons. Shit.

I went back to the main floor and recast my wards. I layered traps on top of traps, painting protections and alarms and nasty little surprises on everything I could reach. I needed a safe place, and this building was it. My arms ached by the time I made it back to the office, brewing up yarrow and wormwood in a pot on the single-coil element Edith swore would burn the whole office down one day. I painted every handkerchief in the box, though I probably only needed one.

Edith came in as I was loading my gun. She stopped in her tracks and bit her lip, watching as I traded ordinary lead for something more potent, courtesy of the wooden box from my safe.

"You've got trouble."

I looked up. "Baby, it's okay."

She eyed the bullets like they would jump off the desk and bite her. "How bad is it?"

She hovered just out of reach, not wanting to come closer. I'd etched each of these bullets with markings so tiny, I had to engrave between breaths. Every one was covered in sigils and symbols, balancing the markings so I wouldn't lose accuracy when I had to shoot. They were magical artifacts, these little instruments of death, and I was pretty sure they would work.

I slipped one into the cylinder and tried smiling. "I want you to stay here this weekend. Here in this building. Don't put a toe outside—I've got the place warded all the way up to the roof. There's nowhere safer in all of Chicago."

Edith closed her eyes. "I thought you were turning this job down."

"I did too," I said. "But I was already in it. Will you stay here?"

"I can't miss my hour at Saint Stanislaus. I have to attend Mass. I should—"

"It's demons," I said. "I'm caught in the middle of a demonic turf war."

She crossed herself. "How—Demons? How did this become about demons?"

"It's the victims." I pulled out another revolver from my desk. "Every one of them found success about ten years ago. They made deals with a devil, and somebody's making off with their souls just before their bill comes due."

Edith bit her lip and looked away. "And your client cares about that. Why?"

I never lie to Edith. Not when I didn't have to. "Because Marlowe's a devil herself. It's her souls that are being stolen."

Edith thumped her clenched fists against her thighs. "I shouldn't have pushed you. You were right not to take this job, and I—What can I do?"

Stay out of trouble. Please God, keep her safe while I do this. "If I'd known this morning, I'd have asked you to get me some holy water. I'm running low."

"It's too late to back out now, isn't it?" She wasn't asking—her voice was as flat as a pancake. Guilt and fear smeared over her face, and I stopped what I was doing to hug her for a minute. She hung on like I was going to disappear.

When she relaxed enough to let go, I drew her closer to the desk. "If you have to leave, you'll need protection. Will you carry my spare revolver?"

She pressed her lips shut and cast a troubled look at the engraved bullets. "Do I have to?"

"You don't have to, but I'd feel a lot better if you did. Demons go in for collateral damage. Pull up a chair and I'll show you how they work."

A swivel stool on wheels rested in the corner. Edith rolled it over and sat, close enough to see but too far to touch.

I held one up and showed her the engraving on the bullet's nose. "Each bullet is molded from iron, not lead. But not just any iron. This stuff came from a meteor. They were quenched in an infusion of angelica, galangal, and rue. It has to be done on a Saturday during the hour of Mars, begun while the moon's void of course—"

Edith fought a smile. "You're doing it again."

"I'm sorry, baby. It just means they're demon-stoppers. I use a low-caliber weapon so the slug's less likely to go through and through, so the bullet can do its work."

"And you want me to carry one of your guns. I hate guns."

"I know. But if you don't have it, and something happens to you—"

Edith sighed. "All right. Load it for me?"

She could load her own gun. I'd taught her. But I wasn't going to push her so much as an inch. I pinched up a slug and slid it into the chamber, one following the other until every chamber was full, the percussion caps gleaming, every one of them engraved with the spell that would activate when the hammer struck it.

It should work, but I couldn't know. I'd never shot a demon before. I'd given up on that plan five years ago.

"Now, if you have to shoot, you shoot, got it? Not just once. Keep firing, all six. Aim for the body and fire until you run out of bullets. Make them dead-dead."

Edith took the revolver from me, but it was clear she didn't want to touch it, from the way it dangled from her fingertips. "It's ugly."

Damn me for getting her into this mess. "I know, baby. But this is too dangerous. I would send you out of town if I could."

"I wouldn't go and you know it." She opened her handbag and rummaged up some space for the gun, but she struggled to shut the clasp. "I can't let anyone see it at work."

"Awkward to draw from your purse, but all right. Keep it on you or near you all the time." I put my thumb in the deep dimple right in the middle of her chin and turned her face toward me. "It could save your life."

The look she gave me was full of regret. "I didn't know. I didn't know it would be this dangerous—"

I kissed her quiet. "It's okay. It'll be okay. Come and help me with those pictures. The last one I shot needs your touch. Then we'll go to Joe's and get a meal while the prints dry; what do you say?"

She sniffed and nodded. "All right. What happened to the photo?"

"Moon came out in the middle of the exposure." I shied away from thinking about what came after, about the look in Ted's eyes when he told me that his life was none of my business. Instead, I tuned in on my worry and chanted, *Please let her be all right,* dropping a mask over my thoughts.

"Hey," Edith said. "I'll be fine. I'm with you."

"That's good. This is the most demon-proof building in Chicago right now, I figure. Now I'm going to teach you a verse you probably didn't learn in catechism class. You need this one on your lips, trust me."

She popped one of my Chesterfields in her mouth and lit up. "Let's hear it."

"Repeat after me: *I exorcise thee, most vile spirit . . .*"

5

EDITH HAD BEEN a shutterbug before I ever met her, and she developed all the pictures her family took in a tiny closet in her old family home. She preferred my darkroom, which was big enough to swing your elbows in. She dragged on the last inch of her cigarette, one hand out for the negative. I handed it over and she held it to the light, squinting through smoke. "It's not so bad. I'll dodge it a little, and we'll see what we get. Want me to print the rest, too?"

"Please."

She crushed out her smoke and pulled the light-chain, plunging us into the dark for a moment before the other lamp switched on. "Pass me the paper."

We were off, working in concert under photo-safe red light. She was the magician, and I was her familiar. We set to our tasks side by side, in the harmony of having worked together for years.

"Mark," she said, and I twisted the timer while she slid the 8x10 into the developer bath. She set up the next exposure while I watched the picture bloom into being. We kept everything moving. I washed the prints and hung them up while she timed the exposures down to the second, as precise as any ritual I'd ever witnessed among the Brotherhood.

She paused over a photo, watching the shadows and light form into the ritual circle and its gory sigils. "This was her blood?"

"Yeah."

"That's one dilly of a spell, Helen. I don't have to be one of your Brothers of the Compass to know that."

Maybe I should have taught her magic. Maybe she would consent to learn it, now that we had time. "You'd have made a good mystic, you know."

She waved one hand. "They don't take women who didn't have male relatives in the order, you said."

That was true. "But your father had the knack. If he'd been with the chapter in Warsaw, you would have started training before you were out of short dresses."

"It doesn't matter. My little knack comes in handy, and you can teach me, can't you?"

I could. We'd start with magical computations and tarot. I could teach her everything I had learned and invented. Years stretched out in front of me, if I got this job done—

Wait. How in the blazes was I supposed to find the White City Vampire, anyway? All I knew was that he was a demon, and how was I going to find a demon in Chicago if Marlowe couldn't do it herself?

She didn't expect me to. I was due to punch out come Monday, making it his deadline as well as mine. If I didn't find him, I could be assured that he would find me first.

The timer chimed. I pulled the print from the stop bath and rinsed it. Edith started the last one in the enlarger, paying it particular attention as she dodged it. "But if Father had been of the Brotherhood, if I had gone to train as a mystic . . . would we have met? Would we have . . ."

If she'd been a Mystic of the Compass, I wouldn't even be dirt on her shoe. She would know what I'd done to be expelled. She would never look at a warlock the way she looked at me now— like I was everything, in that way I didn't deserve.

"Helen." She reached out to caress my cheek. "Look at me."

It was a joy to look at her, and I never got used to the soft, loving shine in her eyes.

"You're wonderful, sweetheart. Don't let anybody knock you down. To Hell with them all. Okay?"

Edith, oh, Edith. She believed in me, and I could never let her know how badly I needed that. "Okay."

Edith shot me a smile and handed me the print.

It was the last one, and she came to stand on my right to take over washing. When the last shot was hanging on the drying line, she studied the print she'd dodged, a little line between her brows. Her whole posture altered, and it made me hold my breath. She slung her jaw forward as a storm gathered in her face, her brow set low over squinting eyes and stern lines from the corner of her mouth. I'd never seen her look like that. She looked—

Violent.

"Edith?"

Nothing.

My voice rose. "Edith?"

She shook herself and came back to me with an apologetic smile. "Sorry. Got lost in thought."

"You sure did."

But she stood at the line and inspected every shot, chewing on the inside of her cheek.

"I don't like this," she said. "I don't like it one bit."

"That makes two of us. You don't have to look at those— Whoa! Where are you going?"

The light from outside the darkroom glowed all around her, and then she was at the coat rack and reaching for her hat. "I've got to go back to Saint Stanislaus."

I followed her out of the darkroom. "What for?"

She tapped her temple and looped her scarf around her neck. "Mrs. Kowalski had something come up. I'm taking her hour with the sacrament."

"You got a brainwave about Mrs. Kowalski, and now you're just going to go?"

"Helen." Edith shrugged her coat into place. "It's the sacrament."

It was special to her. I already knew that, knew she couldn't really explain why it mattered so much. And I knew if I tried to forbid her, even though the idea of her leaving my sight made my throat quiver . . . No. She made her own decisions. "Will you come back?"

"I'll come back." She hung her handbag in the crook of her elbow. "If something comes up, I'll call."

"Got the exorcism memorized?"

She came back to me and gave me a kiss. "I'll bring back some holy water, okay?"

"Good idea." I held on, just for a second. One more kiss.

She pivoted away, the hem of her coat swinging as she laid her hand on the doorknob. "You'll be safe here?"

"Safe as houses, baby. I need to do another augury in"—I glanced at my watch—"twenty minutes. I better do it in the darkroom. The photos aren't as good as the actual site, but they will do."

That satisfied her somewhat, and she slipped out, letting the door click shut behind her. I watched her shadow through the frosted glass, listened for the chime of the elevator, and waited for the sound of the car lurching into motion before I went back into the darkroom to run the spell.

I had a few minutes to kill, and I took out the negative I hadn't let Edith see, the one of my brother that would have prompted questions I didn't want to answer. I had shot it on impulse. The exposure looked good enough, though, and so I slipped it into the enlarger and cast its image onto paper, guided by silver and—sentimentality, honestly. I stood and watched the image bloom, frowning over a defect in the exposure.

I'd caught Delaney in the photo, and I thought he must have been moving when I clicked the shutter open, because his face was blurred. But then I put the print in the stop bath, and I saw the shine on his eyes, as if a mirror lurked behind his pupils to reflect the camera's flash back at the lens. Those eyes shone like a deer caught in headlights, just before a shocked driver wrenched the wheel to the left, right into the path of an oncoming truck—

I backed away, turning to open my file cabinet. I let the drawer strike me in the stomach as I riffled through the files, found the one I wanted, and pulled a print from it. Edith, in a silk slip and stockings, looking at me as she held a match to the end of one of my smokes, the light from the window falling on half her face. It would have been a perfect photo, except for the eyes, shining like mirrors as they caught the flash.

I'd never ever seen that glitch before Edith. But there was Delaney with the same shine. Why?

I washed the print. I hung it up. I'd have to hide it before Edith came back, so I moved a stool and plugged in a fan to help speed it up. The dodged photo fluttered in the breeze, but I caught the bottom edge and stared at it, the augury forgotten.

I had taken the shots with the aim of recording the crime scene to examine later, and then the moon came and I was so busy being interrupted that I hadn't seen it. But I saw it now.

On the ground at the very edge of the frame were footprints, tracking blood away from the ritual circle—and just a few feet up, on the bricks that made the corner of the butcher shop, a smear that could have come from a hand.

The White City Vampire had left a trail.

6

THE GLASS LITTERING the alley had been swept up, the light-bulbs replaced, but I didn't need to take pictures today. What I needed was a scraping of Kelly McIntyre's blood. I had to go over the bricks with a flashlight and a magnifying glass before I scored. It had dried to flakes, so I had to make them stick to the tip of my pendulum with a swipe of K-Y Jelly.

I hadn't researched this spell as thoroughly as the luminous-blood spell, but it was simpler. A little blood on the plumb, and the principles of sympathy would attract like to like—a bit like a dowsing rod, but if I said that to anyone from the Brotherhood, they'd scoff at me for trucking with folk magic.

Well, tally-ho. I pulled my knit cap down over my earlobes, took off my right glove with a frosty sigh, and held the end of the chain.

"Blood of the departed, call to the blood spilled in this place."

The pendulum had barely started swinging before the shadow of a man fell on the wall. I had my hand behind my back so fast one would think I was hiding a cookie. My startled fright did a loop-de-loop as Ted walked into a pool of light.

I let out a sigh and braced myself. *Get away from here,* he would say. *Get away from me, you damned thing.* He might even turn me in, and that would be a real wrinkle. But he kept walking, closer and faster until he caught me in his arms and swept me right off my feet, squeezing so tight, my heart knocked against my ribs.

Ted. My brother, gone for so long, holding me so close I could smell the spicy traces of his aftershave, feel his breath moving through his lungs. Ted. He was there, warm and alive and holding me so tight, I was going to cry if he didn't let me go—I could feel it burning in my nose, and there was no time for blubbering.

"Ow." I wiggled against his grip.

"Shut up." Ted held on. "Just let me—If I'd let you die with those words in your ears, I would have carried that to my grave."

My cheek scraped against the rough wool of his felted coat. "So, you forgive me?"

"No. I don't forgive you. But you're my sister. And you shouldn't be here."

"I have to be here," I said. "I've got a job."

"It's too dangerous. I barely kept Delaney from dragging you to the Grand Lodge and calling for a meeting of the Perfect."

Even outside in the middle of January, I went cold when I heard it. I had stood before the Perfect once. They had declared me warlock and cast me out. I wouldn't bet on being that lucky a second time. "How'd you stop him?"

"I owe him a favor," Teddy said. "Why are you chasing this? You're going to die in two days."

"Not if I get this done. And since you're here, we can put our heads together and—"

Now he let me go. "No. You're not a Mystic of the Compass anymore."

"They don't own all magic. Besides, I've developed spells that would make the Brotherhood scream like girls if they knew what I could do."

Ted jammed his hands inside his pockets. "So, does that mean you're a warlock for real?"

His words froze in little clouds in the air.

"You think I'd go dark?"

He shuffled one foot. "The left-hand path rewards its followers handsomely."

It struck me like a punch. "You'd think that of me. Your own sister."

"I know what you did, sister."

"And you know why."

One side of Ted's mouth turned down. "Intent doesn't absolve you. You became one more paving stone on the road to Hell."

"Ted, listen. This job will save me. If I track down the White City Vampire, I get my soul back."

That stopped him.

He stared at me, his face moving between the stations of his reaction—a shocked jaw falling away from his upper teeth. Eyebrows floating so high, his forehead was ruched like a satin gown, then falling as his nose wrinkled. That was when he realized what that had to mean about my employer, I bet. But it passed in a flicker of hope, a held breath that made me stop my own.

But he looked away before he swung his attention back to me, and I knew what he would say before he said it.

"Even if you succeed, you're still going to Hell."

"But not yet."

"You only have two days."

"That's why I need your help. Why's the Brotherhood of the Compass so keen on this?"

"It's a higher-order affair. Third degree and above."

I smiled. "Third degree already? You're a Magus? That's great—"

"Don't change the subject. If your soul is on the line, I know who you're dealing with." He stuck out his jaw, like he used to when he didn't want to milk the cows or conjugate Latin verbs. "You're in bed with a demon."

I couldn't flinch, so I shrugged. "The completion bonus is hard to resist."

Ted tilted his head back and rolled his eyes at the stars. "The trouble with you is you can't accept fate."

"And neither should you."

He squared off in front of me, feet planted in the snow and arms akimbo. "Haven't you learned when enough is enough?"

"Keep your hair on, little brother. You'll go gray."

He didn't smile back. "You have no idea what you're dealing with. You don't think past the next moment. You don't think of what's going to happen to you—you're going to Hell! Because you wouldn't let me go." He stopped, his face drawn into furious tension. "I was in Heaven. We were all in Heaven. Me, Mom, Dad—"

They had been gone in an instant. The car had been a twisted ruin, the truck in marginally better shape, but the driver of the truck had been slumped over the steering wheel. The deer watched me struggle out of the car, flicked an ear at me, and then bounded away. I was alone on that road. I was going to be alone forever. They were gone, snatched from me in a handful of seconds I would never forget.

I couldn't bear it.

I dragged myself across the rutted snow. I gritted my teeth against the hot throbbing pain in my head, crawling when I couldn't reach the crossroads on my own two feet. I knew how to get them back—and when the demon would only let me choose one, I chose Ted.

He told on me the moment we were alone with our mentors. I didn't blame him. He had been only fourteen, and he believed in the rules. Had he grown up and learned that you had to break rules when they did more harm than good?

I had.

"I would do anything for you. And I did."

"You thought I wanted you to die for me?"

I bit back my words and tried again. "Don't you remember what I said? I don't have to die. Didn't you get that part?"

He clenched his jaw. "I heard you."

"So, help me, why don't you? I've got a lead to chase. Don't you want to see where it goes?"

"Maybe you can't," Teddy said. "I tried to conjure her spirit the other night. No luck."

I held up the pendulum. "I had something else in mind. Killer left a blood trail. You want in or not?"

"You invent that spell?"

"I sure did."

Ted raised his chin and stroked it with one gloved hand. "Fraser always said he hadn't seen an auspex like you in years. He said you were a trailblazer. He'd love to hear about this."

I didn't want Fraser's compliments. "You can't tell him, Teddy. If he knows you worked with me—"

"You think I don't know that?" His eyebrows smoothed out and he nodded. "Go ahead. Do your spell."

"I don't know how this is going to work, exactly. But here goes."

Ted was polite enough to ignore me as I whispered the words that activated the spell. But he turned around when I yelped in surprise. The plumb didn't swing. It pointed, straining at the chain. That defied physics. That was . . .

"Wow."

"Yeah," Ted agreed. "It's like a pointer dog."

Ted had always wanted a dog of his own. I moved my feet, following where the plumb pointed. It didn't care about the buildings in the way. It shifted as I moved so it could keep pointing, and I wondered how far we'd have to go, how I would pass this off if anyone saw us.

Ted walked by my side, just as I promised him we would when he was seven and the Brotherhood of the Compass had taken me away to train. I told Ted secrets when I came home for Christmas, taught him little magics I probably shouldn't have known. But he was going to be one of us. When he was old enough to come to the chapterhouse, it would be me and him. A Sorcerer and his Mystic. A team, always. If I caught this demon, maybe we could walk side by side again someday.

I wondered if I could tell him the truth about me and Edith.

This wasn't the time to wonder about what might be. We had a trail to follow. We moved in step past darkened shops and parked cars. This part of town rolled up the sidewalks at six. Lights glowed in the apartments above the shops, but no one peered out the window at us. They kept to their homes, cozy and warm and listening to *Everyman's Theater* on the radio. The pendulum pointed down the sidewalk and to the corner, where the plumb went wild. It spun in circles right over a point in the middle of a crosswalk.

"This is where the trail ends."

Ted bent at the waist to peer down at the road. "Like he collapsed?"

"And didn't get back up," I agreed. "But how could that be?"

Ted scanned the street. "Why come this way, though? What's here?"

I shrugged. Warm air fled from the collar of my coat. "The phone booth on the corner? A getaway car?"

I scanned the shops. Peckham and Birch Shoes, van Horne Fashions on the corner, Morrison's Fine Cigars in the middle of the street. I moved to the center of the road and emptied my mind, looking for a sign—

"Helen!"

Ted yanked me out of the way. A motorist swerved around us, honking his horn and yelling. Ted hauled me all the way to the sidewalk before he grabbed my shoulders, his face white. "What the hell do you think you're doing?"

"Trying to find a hint."

"In the middle of the road?" he huffed. "You need a keeper."

"You gonna watch over me, Ted?"

He ignored that and pointed. "Why's it riveted to that spot? Is there a spirit?"

I shoved the pendulum in my pocket. It tugged at the seams, attracted to the traces of blood left on the road. I'd have to refine the incantation. "No. There wasn't at the murder scene, either."

If I could just consult him about the sigils . . . he might know. But yapping about the case wasn't part of the deal. He could help me, if I could trust him not to tell.

"You don't have to tell me anything you don't want to." Ted said. "In fact, maybe you shouldn't."

"Brother," I said, imagining Judy Garland and her companions skipping and dancing through a field of poppies. "Manners."

Ted spread his hands, tilting his head toward one shrugged shoulder. "You still think loudly."

"Still."

"I'm just saying I understand the need to keep things secret. Now, what about this dead end?" Ted frowned in thought. "What if it was an accident? He could be in a hospital somewhere."

"That's something I can't learn without greasing the right cop." I eased my glove back on my frozen hand. "Look. I know the Brotherhood has a stake in this."

Ted turned his face away.

I went on. "I don't want to get in your way, but I can't just walk. So, will you work with me? We'll keep it between us."

Teddy's mouth pinned back. "Helen . . ."

"Don't answer now. You know where to find me?"

"I read all your letters."

My chest tingled with warmth. "You could write back, you know. Maybe after this—"

"I have to go." He made good on his words with a heel turn, walking away from me.

He read all my letters.

"You know where to find me," I called after him.

Teddy's shoulders hunched up higher, blocking the wind.

ACT III

1

BY THE TIME WMAQ signed off for the night, I was pacing through my rooms, watching out the windows for Edith's car. My clock brought its hands together at midnight, and I tried to remember prayers I hadn't spoken since I was a child. The empty spot where Edith had parked her late father's Model C gathered snow, the window icy against my forehead.

I found a dry scarf, shrugged into my coat, and stuffed one of the silk handkerchiefs in my pocket. If she wasn't at Saint Stanislaus, if something had happened—

(I've got nothing to promise you, I've got nothing to give, but *please*—)

The phone rang.

I leapt for it. "Edith?"

"It's me."

I caught myself on the wall. "Edith, oh, thank God."

"Don't worry about me. I got caught in a discussion with Father Benedict. He's asking my opinion about the chapel restoration. The sketches are so beautiful."

Edith was caught in conversation. That's all. She was safe. "You scared me to death. I was just about to go looking for you."

"I know; I'm sorry. Is it all right if I borrow your camera to take pictures for the records? I said I would, but the camera you bought me will do if you can't spare yours."

"Of course." Anything. "When are you coming home?"

Her voice faded, as if she had turned her mouth away from the receiver. "I'm going to sing matins with them. Don't wait up."

"I will if I like."

"Stop fretting, Mother."

Someone could hear us, then. "Come home soon."

"I love you," she said, and hung up.

I felt rubbery and relieved, but I jumped at every little sound the office made. My liquor cabinet stored a half-full bottle of bourbon. A generous tumbler joined me on a trip to the record player. Gershwin tickled at the edges of my mind, and the best way to cure a phantom song was to listen to it, all seventeen minutes.

Soon, the opening clarinet fluttered in the air. I swayed, bourbon in hand as I watched the spinning black record, hypnotized by the magic pouring from the needle. Clarinet and piano wove around my head. Edith was coming home and everything was okay. I poured another drink, lit a smoke, and stretched out on my scroll-armed camel-back sofa. The upholstery was stained, worn through on the center cushion, bur it creaked amicably under my back. My copy of *The Great Gatsby* sat on the coffee table, and I picked it up to read about Jay watching the flashing green light across the water.

Jay Gatsby knew a lot about hope. Hope felt a little painful, on account of it not being a sure thing. In fact, there was almost no hope for him, which made that tiny flashing light all the more precious. I'd read this book a dozen times, two dozen. I always held my breath, waiting for Daisy to come to him. Jay hoped every single time, and I hoped right along with him, even though I knew the end.

The bourbon bottle was empty. My clock clicked one, and Edith would be home any minute. I rested the book on my chest and thought about how Edith was better than Daisy any day, while I closed my eyes to the scrape and click of the needle bumping against the record label.

I woke up with a crick in my neck and the odor of the wind in summer just before lightning strikes an open field. Edith stood in my parlor, still wearing her coat. I got up on one elbow and the room tilted, but I didn't mind.

I reached out my hand. "Edith."

She turned toward the record player and lifted the needle off the label. My insides leapt in a dreadful shudder. The movement was wrong. Not like her. By the time she turned to face me I had my revolver out, hammer back and barrel pointed.

That wasn't Edith.

"I exorcise thee, most vile spirit—" Words I knew by heart, spilling from my mouth with thoughtless ease.

"Be not afraid, Elena Brandt."

That wasn't Edith's voice. It scraped the depths of Edith's throat, alien and other. A voice of Hell, and not her body.

"—uproot thyself in the name of our Lord, Jesus Christ, and to flee hence from the voice of God—"

The creature inside Edith's body lifted a hand and swept it to one side, barely stirring the air. My persuader went right along with it, threatening only my bookshelf.

"It is He Himself who commands thee, He who ordered thee to fall from the heights of the heavens to the depths of the earth—"

Every light in the room flared to life. I squinted at Edith's face. She looked back at me impassively, her expression devoid of human feeling. The lightbulbs exploded in a shower of sparks. Light flooded through my windows, burning flashbulb-hot, and her shadow writhed, reaching to the ceiling in a black spread of half a dozen wings.

"I say to you again, be not afraid."

Too late for that. "You're not Edith. Who are you?"

"Haraniel."

Haraniel. Not a name I knew, but I'd be no kind of magician if I didn't recognize a name like that when I heard one.

An angel. An actual soldier of God, here, checking Marlowe's pawn easy as breathing. Angels were real—they were real. Darkness fell, and green spots danced in front of my eyes, and only one thing mattered. "What have you done with Edith?"

"She's here." The creature in Edith tilted her head. "I need your help. You seek a murderer."

This wasn't happening. I couldn't hunt someone for an angel and a demon at the same time. "That's real sweet, but my dance card's a little full at the moment."

"Edith is asking me to explain. She's sorry she didn't tell you before."

"Tell me what, that she's an angel?"

"Edith is a woman. A . . . host." Edith's hands rose and I cringed at their stilted gesture and the awkward flump of Edith's limbs as the angel sighed. "I have never before controlled the flesh. It's . . . disorienting."

The wrongness twitched over my skin. That was Edith's face but harsher, her expressions grim and heavy with judgement, but I knew in my bones—that wasn't her. The angel—he? She? Did angels think of themselves as women, or men, or was it meaningless to them?

This wasn't the time to wonder. I looked them in the eye, and even the way they gazed at me was different. "You're possessing her."

"With her consent. She's a very godly woman."

"If you forgive the perversion."

Haraniel grimaced. "The revulsion for homosexual love is a human prejudice. How you perform intercourse is irrelevant. Edith keeps love in her heart. She's generous. She is more merciful than I."

"I get the picture. So, what, you took Edith over, and—how long have you been watching her?"

"Edith and I have been together for a long time, Elena. Longer than you've known her."

My jaw hung down so low I was catching flies. "Together? You mean—"

"Edith has the power to contain me and has consented to guide me through my displacement and my penance."

"Displacement . . ." *and penance,* they said. It clicked. "You're one of the angels who fell."

"We didn't fall," Haraniel corrected. "We were expelled from Heaven for our arrogance. Hundreds of us were all evicted."

"Why?"

Haraniel shrugged. "That's a long story."

My hand found my pack of Chesterfields. I shook one out and lit it, rubbing at my eyes. "Okay, let's go back. You . . . ride along in her body. When we, I mean when me and Edith—"

"When you make love."

I looked away. "So, you're there? When we—um."

"I absent myself, though I am to some degree aware of Edith's physiology at all times."

"So, you know about the—"

"Yes."

I covered my face and hoped I was dreaming.

"I assure you, Edith enjoys it a great deal."

I had to turn away. I couldn't look an angel in the eye when they blithely talked about—about our private business.

"I'm not hearing this," I said. "Skip it."

When I peeked back, Haraniel was still standing there, their posture oddly static, staring me right in the face. I glanced away. I looked back.

Haraniel hadn't even twitched an eyelash.

"All right," I sighed. "I'm going to forget we even had this conversation. New subject. Edith didn't tear out of here to pinch-hit for Mrs. Kowalski. It was to do with the pictures, wasn't it?"

"Yes. I need you to find the White City Vampire, Elena."

First demons, then the Brotherhood, now angels—who wasn't looking for this guy? "Peachy. What for?"

"He has to be stopped. You saw the markings in the picture."

"You mind telling me what they are?"

Haraniel tilted Edith's head. Not Edith, again. Haraniel stopped at the wrong angle. "Can you tell me what purpose a ritual serves through the drawing of its space?"

What kind of a question was that? Were they stalling, or did they actually want to know? Didn't matter. "Not that one. The markings in the photographs are strange. I feel like I've seen them before, but I don't know where." I blew out smoke. "Now, either they're invented and we're out of luck, or . . . shit."

Haraniel had the knack of raising one eyebrow. Edith couldn't do that. "Or?"

"Or the information is so obscure, you'd only find it in the hands of a group like the Brotherhood of the Compass."

"The Brotherhood that expelled you."

"Exactly."

"Then securing their help isn't an option. Can we go back to the site of Kelly McIntyre's murder?"

"The Brotherhood is watching it."

"Perhaps an older scene. Or—"

Haraniel froze, turning to stare out the windows. Birds gathered on the sills, dodging and fluttering in a dark-feathered mass. Edith's body sighed, and Haraniel pressed their lips together. "Get your coat. And your camera. There's been another murder."

2

THE ROOM SPUN under my feet. I teetered and threw my arms out to balance against the force, but I landed on the sofa with a thump.

"You're drunk."

"I was thirsty."

Haraniel huffed in exasperation and reached for me. I shied away but they planted their hand on my pate, fingers spread. A brief flash of pain later, my head cleared.

"Drink a tall glass of water," Haraniel said.

"What did you do to me?" Even as I asked, I jumped to my feet. "Wait. I have to—"

I all but ran for the bathroom. I was sober as a judge, but I bent over the tap to drink handfuls of water after I'd soaped them clean. I felt like I'd gotten a full night's sleep and a cup of coffee after. My mind was clear and alert. How did they do it?

"I dragged the toxins out of your blood and flushed them through your kidneys."

I jumped back from their reflection in the dusty mirror. "Yaa!"

Haraniel stood in the bathroom with me, laden with my coat, my hat, and my Graflex. "Drink more water."

"How did you—"

They thrust the coat at me. The pockets bulged with film magazines and Sashalites. It made the hair on my neck stand up to watch them move, so uncanny, east of human. "Translocation is a process of dismantling the atoms that make up a physical body and attendant objects and reassembling them in the location you wish."

I stuffed one arm in my jacket. "Okay, pretend I didn't understand that."

Were they smirking at me? "I teleported. We have to hurry."

The frosted window in the bathroom was shadowed by the beat of a host of black wings. My back crawled at the sound. "Hurry where?"

"To the murder, Elena. It woke the birds. They're upset."

"How do you know that?"

"Every time I feed one, I tag it with a particle of my consciousness. It seemed useful." They stepped forward and helped my arm into the other sleeve.

Edith must have fed a thousand birds. More. "Where are we going?"

Haraniel looked up at the ceiling, and for a moment they were just like Edith, reckoning something in her head. "The zoo. I think it's at the zoo. More of them are awake there. Button your coat; it's snowing. I forgot your galoshes."

They vanished. I was still gaping at the space where they'd been when they returned to it, kneeling to help me put on rubber overshoes.

"Come on, I can dress myself," I grumbled, but they guided my heel into place. They took my hand and we dissolved.

I never realized how much I was a body until I didn't have one, how deeply I was my conscious thought until it disappeared, and I was nothing and nowhere and not. And then I was, and that was when I became afraid.

I yanked out of the angel's grip. I staggered away and didn't stop until I was well out of reach. I had been nothing. Nothing. It wasn't like falling asleep. It wasn't like falling asleep at all.

"Haraniel." My stomach lurched, but I didn't get sick, thank God. "Never do that to me again."

"It's a long walk back to the Reliance Building."

"So, I'll walk it. That was horrible."

"It's not that bad." Haraniel turned in a circle. "That way. The birds there are agitated."

Fresh-fallen snow crunched under their feet. I sank into a drift and gritted my teeth. Snow trickled over the edge of my boot top, but I kept on. The shadows took on weird shapes ahead of us. Birds flew past me and lighted on the skeletal branches of trees—gray-blue jays, little sparrows, pigeons and grackles all flocked together, feathers be damned.

"Haraniel?"

The angel had stopped walking, their head bent as they looked at something lying in the snow.

I caught up to them then, and the sight made me turn away to empty my stomach.

Blood painted the snow in intricate detail, a pentagram within a heptagram bounded by a triple circle. Within the rings, sigils glistened. The body in the center of it all steamed, warm and still and staring and so, so red. He was big, cushioned with the fat that barrels up the body of a strong man once he hits forty and stops smashing heads. He was naked as a jaybird, lying spread-eagle in the middle of the circle painted in his own blood. In the center of his chest was a square of those same letters I didn't recognize from the alley.

Blood stained a circular dent in the snow between his spread-eagle legs. A perfect circle, like a bowl had rested there, positioned to catch blood from a neat wound in his upper thigh. Femoral artery. He would have exsanguinated in no time.

So, that's why the papers called him Vampire.

The body was still warm. But I suspected what would happen even as I stripped off my glove and let the pendulum swing from my bare fingers. "Spirit of this man, speak with me."

The plumb lay still.

"Shit."

The connection between a body and its soul lingers for three days, in normal circumstances. His should have been right there, but it wasn't.

Had this guy dealt with Marlowe for his fondest wish? It was safe to guess yes. But Marlowe said I was next. Why had the White City Vampire skipped over me?

"We have to hurry," Haraniel said.

Pictures. Get the pictures. I opened the Graflex and got to work, adjusting the shutter speed and the f-stop for flash photography—no need for my luminous blood spell there. As I put the camera to my eye, the grisly scene flipped upside down and backward, becoming a framed image. A little farther away, a little less real.

My routine for photographing scenes scoured away the edges of the horror and the winter stink of murder. North. East. South. West. I moved around the scene like a wind-up doll: shoot, slide the shield over the exposure, flip the cartridge or pocket it for a new one, unscrew the flashbulb, replace it with fresh. Burnt filament and blood tickled up my nose, the odor clinging to my senses.

The routine kept me from screaming. It kept me from really seeing what sprawled out before me—human sacrifice, the darkest of the dark arts, the work of Hell and all its devils. I was working for one, no matter how charming she was, no matter how interesting the work she gave me turned out to be. I was knee-deep in darkness, and I never, never wanted another job like this. I was collecting my soul, we were going west, and Edith would be our breadwinner. I was finished. No more work like this, not ever again.

Wingbeats cut the air as birds gathered around Haraniel, lighting on the ground at their feet and calling from branches overhead. The flock landed on whatever would hold them, chattering to each other. Not a one of them crossed the first bloody ring where the body lay among the markings in the snow, their delicate tracks neatly skirting the boundaries.

Tracks.

I studied the churned-up snow. There was the print of my rubbers, a stack of chevrons across the instep and heel. There were the marks Haraniel made with Edith's shoes—four pointed stars alternating like polka dots, the heels scuffed down.

Inside the circle were other footprints. Wavy lines across the sole. Petite, with narrow, raised heels. I put it together with the lower eyeline at the alley scene, and it clicked.

"A woman. The White City Vampire's a woman."

It was clever. The right woman could stroll right past a squad of cops rushing to the scene and they'd only stop her to say *go home; it isn't safe.* It didn't matter that the stiff in the snow was two hundred pounds if he was an ounce. A demon could haul that much meat to this spot, no matter what body it was using. Marlowe could probably move the piano across her creamy white hotel suite if she put her mind to it. Would it be possible to—

"Haraniel."

"Yes, Elena?"

"Do demons possess people the same way angels do?"

They twitched, and I could almost see offended feathers ruffling. "Angels enter a mutual agreement. We don't join a host without their consent."

"But demons don't bother to ask."

"Demons have no concern for the moral implications of their actions. They take what they want and leave the host to deal with the demon's crimes, disposing of them like paper tissue."

Marlowe had been the same person every time I met her. Did that woman know what was striding around in her body? Who had she been before Marlowe had taken a fancy to her skin?

Never mind that for now. Haraniel just said that demons hop bodies, and that revelation really put a wrinkle in my turf-war theory, didn't it? If Marlowe's demon competition was jumping from puppet to puppet, we'd have to catch her red-handed.

Coming at me, I imagine.

Haraniel shoved their hands in their pockets. "It's vile, what this demon is doing. Unspeakable."

"I agree," I said. "But why kill like this? Does she need to do it this way to retrieve the souls?"

"Perhaps," Haraniel said. "But the demon could simply enjoy the pain and fear. Trying to gift a demon with reasons behind their actions may not be wise. They do evil because that is what they are."

"Hm."

Haraniel accepted that response as sufficient and turned their attention to a grackle.

I hated every second I spent looking at the scene, but I wound my way around the sigil-filled circle and ceremonial seals, examining every sign, trying to puzzle out the unfamiliar marks and what purpose they served. The body stared up at the sky.

Circles protected. Circles bound. Circles defined a space, cut it away from the physical plane to marry it to the realm where matter was meaningless, where quintessence made the rules. But this magical ground was a jumble sale of manifestations, and I had no time to take the markings apart and decipher their purpose.

It could have been me, lying out there in the snow. Marlowe said I was next in line. Had it been my warded fortress or the presence of an angel that protected me? "Haraniel. Have you noticed anyone sneaking around me or Edith? Anyone at all?"

"Do you think the killer is after you?"

I sighed. "There's a damned good chance I'm—"

"Hey! Hands in the air!"

Big shoulders. Peaked cap, brass buttons, a six-gun straight-armed right at our lives. The grackle leapt from Haraniel's shoulder, its wingbeats loud as a drum.

The gun's nose steadied. The patrolman planted his boots in the snow.

"No!"

I tried to push them out of the way, but Haraniel put Edith's body in front of mine. The shots made them flinch, two three four five bullets just like that, Edith's body jolting as they marched across her coat. The sting of the last one knocked me back a step, washing my ankle in snow. Warm blood spilled down my skin, chilled by the January air seeping into the hole in my coat, but before I could finish thinking *I've been sho*—I was nothing once more, nothing and nobody and nowhere.

3

THE PAIN DIDN'T hit until we dropped out of the outer darkness. I clapped a hand over my shoulder and squeezed, hissing at the aliveness of it. I was real again, and I tilted my head back in reflexive thanks.

Frescoes decorated the arched ceiling of the nave of a church. Saints and angels looked down on me and all I'd done, all I was, and part of me shrank back from their judgement. My life poured out of the hole in my shoulder, but I held on to Edith, tried to keep her from falling.

But Haraniel didn't fall. They stood up steady and true, moving as if nothing had happened.

I had seen it. I had heard the shots. Every time Edith's body flinched at the hits, it had shocked me with horror and grief. She should be dead. But Haraniel stood. They turned to me, laying their hand on my shoulder.

The pain disappeared. Even the hole in my coat mended. Edith would have been dead on the ground after catching that much lead. Haraniel caught my wrist before they sidled between pews.

"But he shot you."

"I took care of it. Sit."

I shook my head. "I have to go. I don't belong here."

They sighed, nostrils flaring, and violet shadowed under their eyes. "All are welcome in the house of God, Elena. Sit down."

The pew was firm and uncomfortable. Haraniel fell into place beside me, one hand on the pew ahead of us as they dropped their head like it was too heavy to hold upright. They closed their eyes and sighed again.

I touched Haraniel's shoulder. "Are you all right?"

"I need a minute."

"Are you hurt? Are you still bleeding?"

"Elena," Haraniel said. "Please be quiet for a few minutes."

I tried not to fidget as the priest sang holy office to an empty church. It was beautiful enough to make an angel cry. Haraniel rested their head on their arm. Edith's face turned toward me, eyes closed, a tiny frown etched between her eyebrows. She was still hurt. I had to get help for her. A doctor. She needed a doctor.

"The singing of lauds is sufficient," Haraniel said. "Please stop fidgeting."

So, they had Edith's trick. Or was it Haraniel's trick all along?

They cracked open an eyelid to shoot me a look. I folded my hands and listened. The priest could have been on the radio. He could have been at the opera house. His voice filled the space in a way that hushed me, even though I wanted to get up and (*flee*) breathe air that wasn't redolent with frankincense, get out of there before they saw me and knew I had no right to be there—

"All are welcome in the house of God, I said."

I closed my eyes and tried not to think too loudly.

The chant ended. The priest was young, my age probably, with a shining face to match his clear voice speaking prayers in Latin. It was the usual *God almighty, have mercy on us* stuff. Haraniel had to shake my shoulder when it was over.

I suppressed a yawn like my life depended on it. "Sorry."

"It's late."

They looked better but not by much. I swiped at my face. "Now what?"

Haraniel rose from the pew and headed straight for an older priest who had observed the service. I tried to hang back, but he stared holes into me, like he could see exactly what I was.

I put my chin up and met his eye. "Fine service, Father."

He squinted for a second before he spoke. "You have an unusual companion, Haraniel."

I raised my eyebrows, but he turned away, gesturing at us to follow. Ice water glided along my nerves as I was led deeper into the church than I wanted to go. "Why are we here?"

"Father Benedict can help us," Haraniel said. "He's a host."

"Him too? How many—oh, shit, not you again."

Waiting in the sacristy, clad in black save a chip of white at their throats, were Ted and his partner, Delaney. Ted kept his eyes on Haraniel—and why not? Edith was a well-made woman. But Delaney's mouth went sour as he snapped his fingers at me. "You. You need to get your nose out of our business."

Father Benedict eyed them and shook his head. "You should have left the costumes at the lodge, gentlemen. Your current attire is a touch disrespectful."

Heh. So much for the sham.

"Our apologies," Ted said. "Sometimes, our work asks us to conceal our identities."

"You know this woman, I take it."

He nodded toward me and I stood up straight. "I'm just—"

"I'm her brother," Ted said. "It's a complicated story. She's meddling in affairs that don't concern her."

"Oh, I'd say I have a right to be concerned," I muttered, but Father Benedict put up his hand. I went quiet, but I tried to push a thought at Ted, in case he was listening: *I have to talk to you.*

He didn't even glance at me. "If we could take a moment of your time—"

"Of course," Father Benedict said. "But I already promised my time to these ladies. I'll be with you in a moment. Take the time to reflect upon deception."

Father Benedict's office was small but full of comforts. Two chairs faced a desk in matching cherry-red stained wood, its surface bare of everything save a blotter, a Bible, and a glossy black pen. You couldn't see the walls for the books, arranged behind glass-fronted doors with locks. I recognized a few spines on the shelf behind the pater's desk, the titles stamped in golden Latin. A parishioner wouldn't give them a second thought, but an eight-pointed star rested on a few of those spines.

Well, well, well.

Father Benedict whispered a phrase as he closed the door. He lifted his hand and traced a sigil in the air, and the room felt a little smaller, the pressure on my eardrums a little firmer. We were warded—against listeners, I bet.

Father Benedict turned to Haraniel with thunder in the set of his jaw, his brow crumpled and low. "Haraniel, why have you brought this damned soul before me?"

Not one to put a gentle edge on it.

Haraniel leaned on the desk, all their weight poised on their fingertips. "She's a private investigator hired to look into the identity of the White City Vampire."

He flicked me an irritated glance. "She knows our business?"

I didn't. But I wasn't about to open my mouth and prove it. "I help where I can. Good works and all that."

He stared me down with fierce, dark eyes. The way he cocked his head made me think of a bird of prey. "You were expelled from the order. Your soul is forfeit. Which came first?"

"Edith tells me you're renovating the chapel where you adore the Eucharist. She's very excited."

"I asked you a question."

My smile was more like a show of teeth. "And I was trying to avoid pointing out how rude it was."

Haraniel stepped between us. "There was another murder, Zashiel."

Father Benedict's—Zashiel's eyebrows jumped up their face. "You're sure?"

"We were at the scene," I said. "Haraniel felt it happen, but I don't know how."

"It was the birds." Haraniel shrugged and turned to Zashiel.

"Elena took pictures of the markings, but they still need to be developed."

Zashiel perched on the edge of their desk. They were better at controlling their host's body than Haraniel was with Edith's. Their movements were smooth, but I could tell the flesh wasn't part of them, even though it fit like a good suit. "I'd like to see the signs and markings used."

"I can get them developing tonight. Or Edith can. She's better at printing than I am." I shot Haraniel a look. "Can Edith come out and play?"

"She's anxious to talk to you," Haraniel said. "For now, we should go."

We should. I was tired, right down to my bones. A booze-soaked snooze wasn't enough to sustain all this teleporting and being shot by cops. I needed to close my eyes, even for an hour.

"I have to see to those gentlemen outside." Zashiel nodded toward the warded door.

"Then I'd better get out of here. They won't work with me."

"I wasn't going to suggest it. But for what it's worth, I wish there were something I could do about your soul."

A little disquieting voice inside me wondered if all angels could see the condition of my soul. And if they could, did Edith know?

I shook it off. She would have asked me. "Thanks, Padre. That's real nice of you to say." I nodded at Haraniel. "We really shouldn't keep your friend any longer."

We walked out of Zashiel's office. Delaney looked at me with dagger-sharp eyes. Ted glanced at me for a heartbeat, then turned resolutely away. He couldn't let on that we'd talked to each other. I knew that.

The cut still sank deep into my gut.

Haraniel led the way until we were out of sight. "I'm getting us out of here."

Oh, no. Not again. I stepped back, but Haraniel was too fast for me. They squeezed my shoulder just before I ceased to exist.

ACT IV

1

WE RE-MANIFESTED IN the same patch of alleyway where I'd begun this case, the sky overhead soft with the rosy touch of dawn. Pigeons stared down at us from old dovecotes, residents of the home they'd known for generations. I took a step back and found a smoke. All this translocation had me on edge.

"What are we doing here?"

"This is where you found the first square." Haraniel glared at the wall, and I half-expected it to straighten up and look smart. "Tell me exactly what you learned from this location."

"You saw the pictures," I said. "Sigils all over the place, written in the victim's blood. Blood tracked away from the summoning site—"

"You know it's a summoning?"

Haraniel made me want to rip my own hair out sometimes. "I don't know! Maybe. I'm guessing. I haven't had a minute to breathe, much less discern the purpose of the configuration."

"I understand. What were you saying about blood tracks?"

"I didn't notice it until the photos. The killer walked away. But she only got as far as the intersection, as far as I can tell. The trail just stops."

The angel in Edith's body turned away and headed for the street.

"Where are you going?"

"Canvassing for witnesses. If someone collapsed in the street, perhaps someone helped them."

"But wouldn't the cops already—Slow down." I trotted to catch up with them. "It's Sunday. All the shops are closed."

"All those shopkeepers are headed to Mass."

They were right. Families in lint-brushed coats and shiny shoes flocked on the early-morning sidewalk, waiting for fathers to bring the cars around. They glanced left and right to make sure people noticed the fine cut of their coats and the well-tended tresses of their daughters, an envy-shadowed smile for the mother who wore the smartest hat.

We waded into the river of Joneses and I took the lead, a smiling, sympathetic face to blunt Haraniel's thunder and judgement.

"How do you do," I said to a woman in a green pillbox. I opened my wallet and showed her my license, but she concentrated on my smile. "Do you know who collapsed in the street in the small hours of Tuesday morning?"

She lifted a gloved hand to her mouth. "I shouldn't say." She glanced at the child hanging off her left hand, gloved in a green that matched her hat. "An awful business. How she managed to escape that fiend, only to—"

She swallowed whatever she was going to say next. I had to be careful with her. She might have seen the woman in the street, covered in blood, and there was no way she didn't connect her to the gruesome scene outside the shop where she bought sausage. This was probably the worst horror of her life, and I was dragging her back into it. I had to step gently, or she'd crack like an egg.

"Was she hurt?" Haraniel asked. "Was there an accident?"

Oh, for Pete's sake.

The woman glanced at the other families gathering in the street. What must they think of her, accosted by strangers on the way to church? "I wouldn't like to speak of it in front of the children."

A sleek Chevrolet prowled up to the curb, and the man driving leapt out with the engine idling. "What's this about, Mildred? Is this woman bothering you?"

"She wants to know about Mathilda," she said. "But the children—"

Mathilda. I filed the name away and turned my attention to the man. "Just a few questions."

"I'll handle it. Get in the car." He had a brutish look about him, even in his Sunday best. Big bare hands with scars across the knuckles. He might knock a woman down on a Sunday, if he thought that woman was troubling his wife. He got into my face, and the odor of cigar smoke wafted off his breath. "What's this about?"

"We're looking for Mathilda's family." Don't stop smiling. "I'm an investigator working for an attorney who believes there's a substantial damage case."

He glanced at Haraniel, then back at me. "Who's hiring women investigators?"

"Mostly, we do interviews and research. Nothing dangerous."

He chewed it over. "Why do you want to see the van Hornes?"

I connected that name to the dress shop on the corner, with the smart ladies' suit and a hat like the one perched on the missus. The killer—the *victim*—must have been on her way back home when she collapsed in the street.

Haraniel spoke up. "We're looking to assess her condition and inform the family of their right to compensation."

That was a damn clever lie. I didn't know the angel had it in them.

"Money in it, eh? Money won't bring Mathilda back."

"But it could help. Money generally does," I said.

"Anything we learn that could help locate the White City Vampire will be reported to the authorities," Haraniel said. "Anything to find that monster."

He let his shoulders sink, easing their tension. "Mathilda has a steady beau. That's probably what she was doing out of bed in the middle of the night. She shouldn't have snuck out, but young girls, love, you know how it is." He looked at the intersection and shook his head. "Whatever she saw that night, it broke her mind, poor thing. Hasn't uttered a word since it happened, though everybody knows anyway."

"Is she at home with her mother?"

He glanced at his watch. "She's up at Dunning."

My stomach shivered. "Maybe they can cure her."

"I don't think so. They found her covered in blood, but otherwise, not a scratch. How she got away from that fiend I'll never know."

Everyone thought Mathilda was another victim—and she was. Just not the way everyone assumed. Why would anyone think a girl would have the strength to subdue a big woman like Nightingale McIntyre?

Had the demon let her go when he was done using her body? Did she wake in that alley, covered in blood, running away from what she'd done—what her body had done while someone else drove?

"Poor girl," I said. "Someone's got to pay for that."

The window of the Chevrolet rolled down. "Fred," the missus said. "We'll be late."

"Coming." Fred looked back at me. "If there's somebody to sue, you sue them, you hear me? Take them for everything. Mathilda was a sweet girl."

He stepped over the slush in the gutter and got inside the car. I glanced at Haraniel, who stared at a bunting without really focusing on it.

"Dunning's a long way north," I said.

"I know where it is. Do you want a cigarette before we go?"

"Not so fast." I swung my shoulder away from their touch. "I've had enough of your teleportation trick. We're taking my car."

2

THE HEATER COUGHED out warm air as I drove my square and sturdy '31 Ford to the state hospital. I didn't like asylums, and I especially didn't like this one, which didn't even have the gothic charm of older nuthouses. This is where they dumped the lost and unwanted—the maniacs, the depressives, the hysterical . . .

And the homosexuals, if I wanted to hit the target. They called it a sickness, but nobody who had vanished from the Wink had ever come back to say they were cured. Funny how nobody they decide is crazy ever seems to get better.

I had no reason to like Dunning.

Haraniel stepped in front of me as we walked into the lobby, asking the nurse at the desk where to find Mathilda van Horne. She took us up to the girl's room, where a well-dressed woman in gray wept quietly while she brushed the buckwheat-colored hair of the girl sitting by the window. The space behind Mathilda's eyes was for rent. Fat, black-throated chickadees gathered on the sill, tiny heads bobbing as they jostled closer to the window, trying to get her notice.

The older woman stopped brushing her daughter's curls. "Can I help you?"

I ducked my head in polite greeting. "Mrs. van Horne? We're sorry to disturb you and your daughter. We're investigators, and we wanted to get an official assessment of her condition."

Mathilda was a beautiful girl. Instead of the shapeless hospital gowns and bathrobes the other inmates shuffled in, she wore a pale blue blouse with dozens of pintucks and tiny buttons, a knife-pleated skirt draped over her knees, expensive powder-blue kid-leather shoes. Her empty eyes were framed by mascara-coated lashes. Her slack mouth was a soft carnation pink, suitable for a young miss. All she lacked was the animation I took for granted in people, but its absence was a chilling, terrible thing.

A shimmering line of drool leaked from Mathilda's mouth. Mrs. van Horne dabbed Mathilda's chin in a gesture she'd already mastered. "She looked at me this morning." Her voice trembled, damp with tears. "When I gave her breakfast. She eats just fine when you feed her. She doesn't like onions in her hash browns."

I nodded. "She looked at you when you fed her hash browns?"

She went back to shaping her daughter's hair. "I shouldn't make such a fuss. It could have been reflex. The doctor says—"

She deflated.

"Never lose hope, ma'am. If onions stimulate her, that can only be a good sign." I kept my smile gentle. "This is my partner, Edith Jarosky."

Haraniel bowed their head in a solemn, respectful nod.

Mrs. van Horne flashed all the cheer she could manage in the circumstances. "How do you do."

"I am sorry for your trouble." I took out my notepad and posted my pen, a Parker Edith had given me last Christmas. "I know this will be painful for you, but if I may ask, do you remember anything unusual about that night? Anything at all."

"I—" A thought flashed. I caught the shine on her eyes, tensing as she pushed it aside. She leaned forward to dab Mathilda's chin. "Nothing."

"It could be that you experienced something that you think no one will believe," I said. "There's often a feeling something isn't right when your loved ones are in danger."

She stayed silent for a long time. She looked at me, and then glanced toward the chickadees. "I had a dream."

Bingo. "What did you dream?"

"I was in the hallway, and Mathilda's door glowed around the cracks. It was so bright. I opened the door and she was bathed in light. I almost couldn't see her. And then she was gone."

Haraniel shifted, the shoulders of their coat rising.

I looked up from my jotted notes. "You had this dream that night?"

"Sometimes, I think it was the angels, taking her away from her suffering," she said. "But that would mean there's no hope, no hope she'll be anything but—"

She folded her hands in her lap and shut her eyes, stopping her tears.

"Do you often dream like that when something happens in your family?" Haraniel asked.

Mathilda's mouth twitched as I stopped myself from glancing Haraniel's way. That was miles better than the ham-handed inquisition they pulled on Mrs. Mildred. It was exactly what I would have asked, mirroring Mrs. van Horne's language to ease into rapport.

Women were gifted more often than men. She probably was clairvoyant: calling them dreams was how she rationalized her power. But no one from the Brotherhood of the Compass would even look at her twice if she didn't have a male relative to serve as a mystic, doing the divination and computations that took too long for true magicians to bother with.

"You'd be surprised how often we hear things like that," I said.

"My mother told me she dreamed the night my father died in Ypres. He stood at the foot of her bed, she said, in his uniform."

"Sometimes, you just know," Haraniel said.

Mathilda turned her head, her eyes still unfocused. She faced Haraniel, mouth parted.

"Mathilda?" Mrs. van Horne said. She looked at Haraniel with wide eyes. "She reacted to your voice. Say something else."

"What should I say?"

Mathilda opened her mouth, lips moving as if she groped for words.

I grabbed at Haraniel's coat. "She's trying to say something. Keep talking."

"Pray for her," Mrs. van Horne said.

Haraniel's gaze darted about, but they sighed. "By the intercession of St. Michael and the celestial Choir of Seraphim—"

Mathilda trembled and took in a deep breath, but her eyes remained empty even as she let out an ear-splitting scream.

3

MATHILDA SCREAMED WHILE a pack of white-clad orderlies hustled us out of the room. She screamed and kicked as they strapped her down. She screamed as the heavy door swung shut on the nurse, needle poised with a drop of sedative glistening at the tip. Mathilda shrieked once more, then went silent.

Mrs. van Horne wept as I steered her down the hall and into a common area bustling with patients. A woman in a holey cardigan over printed pajamas played the first movement of *Moonlight Sonata* slightly off time. She struck a wrong note, cried "No!" and started over, from the top. The other lost souls swayed or sat enfolded in their own mystery, save the one who looked me right in the eye.

I took clammy hands off Mrs. van Horne's shoulder and tried to swallow, but my mouth was a desert. Harriet. Oh, God. She hadn't been around the Wink in the last couple of months. Now I knew why. Dunning had gotten her.

Harriet fingered the cuffs of a chenille housecoat, a soft pastel yellow that framed a dull, powdery green nightdress. I'd never seen Harry in anything less than her dapper, sharp-shouldered best. Who put her here, claiming to love her? Who had committed her to this place, where they would strap her into a device that would deliver electric shocks when she looked too long at a picture of a woman?

They called it aversion therapy. Therapy. I never met anyone who said they were cured.

Harriet sat perfectly still, her mouth shaped around an unspoken word. Then she smiled to break my heart. She got on her feet and shuffled out of the common room on ballet-pink slippers, never looking back.

I hated myself for the relief that dripped over my skin, for the knot in my stomach going slack. Did I know anyone else there? I hoped not.

Three tall north-facing windows provided soft light and the best seats in the house. At the first, a young woman stood unseeing by a window crowded with chickadees. At the second, another girl, plain-faced and indifferently groomed, had a puzzle spread out in front of her to ignore. More birds clamored at her window. At the third, a woman in curlers and an iron-haired grandmother faced each other in a game of chess. Pieces flashed as they moved pawns and stopped the clock. The sill by their side didn't have so much as a stray feather.

"Edith," I said.

Haraniel looked up from their seat at Mrs. van Horne's side. "What?"

"Those two, by the windows."

Haraniel tilted their head, something tiny and bright in their eyes. "What about them?"

A chair scraped across linoleum tile. I looked back.

They had turned to face us. Their empty eyes drove icy tacks into me. The birds chirped and bumbled, pressing closer to the glass.

"Does that mean anything to you?" I asked.

Haraniel pressed their lips together and gave the windows a wary stare, but a doctor clad in a white coat and absolute power stepped right between her and Mrs. van Horne, brandishing a clipboard and a gold Cross pen. He offered her a smooth pink hand, saying, "Mathilda is calm now. No need to worry. As frightening as it was, it's a promising sign."

Mrs. van Horne's lip quivered. "She's all right?"

"Fast asleep."

Drugged to the gills, that meant.

Mrs. van Horne slapped a damp hanky to her face and gasped out one more sob. The doctor removed a triplicate form from his clipboard and held it out.

"Mrs. van Horne, I need you to take this to your husband."

"What's it for?" I asked.

His mouth soured as he took in my rumpled, feminine attire. "And you are?"

"That's her daughter," I said. "Shouldn't she know?"

Mrs. van Horne squinted at the form. "Electroconvulsive therapy? You want to electrocute Mathilda?"

"It's a new treatment," the doctor said, and he had that soft, crooning voice one uses on small children after a nightmare. "I think today proves Mathilda could be brought back from her catatonia with electrical stimulation to her brain."

Mrs. van Horne drew her hand away. "That sounds painful. I don't know."

"Now, now, Mrs. van Horne. That's up to your husband. Don't you want your daughter back home?"

She flicked her gaze to me. "Isn't there something else we could do?"

I came to attention as she looked to me for help. "Tell him about the onions—"

"This is the best treatment for your daughter. I'll explain it all to your husband; don't you worry. Why don't you go home and give him that paper?"

Mrs. van Horne stared at the form an instant longer, then surrendered, one palm out.

"Good girl," the doctor said. He looked at Haraniel and tucked whatever he'd been about to say into a polite little smile. "I have other patients to attend."

He patted Mrs. van Horne's shoulder and strode away. Mrs. van Horne stared at the form in her trembling hand.

"I don't want Mathilda to hurt," she said, searching between Haraniel and me. "Don't you think it would hurt?"

What was I to say to that?

Haraniel stirred then and spoke up. "Perhaps you should see what she's like tomorrow. Perhaps you should ask the kitchen to put onions in her hash browns."

The long furrows in her brow smoothed. Hope kindled in her eyes. "Tomorrow?"

"There's no need to be hasty about a decision like this," I said, and her mouth broke open on a glad little sigh. I smiled at that. "Would you like an escort to your car?"

"Yes. I should go home." She opened her handbag and folded up the form, tucking it down into a side pocket. She pulled out pale gray gloves that matched her shoes, pulling each finger on as if she were in a trance.

"Elena." Haraniel cut a glance toward the window. The girl had shuffled closer. She reached for Haraniel, her mouth moving with incoherent purpose.

"That's Roberta Howard. She hasn't moved an inch since she came here." Mrs. van Horne stepped between them, hands on the young girl's shoulders. "Roberta, Roberta dear. Can you hear me?"

Roberta jerked herself away from Mrs. van Horne with a wordless denial. Mrs. van Horne reached for her again, but Roberta howled and lashed out, bashing her wrist against Mrs. van Horne. She lurched around the obstacle, intent on Haraniel.

I stepped in front of them myself. I was in no shape to tangle with the likes of Roberta, but I didn't want to know what would happen if she laid hands on Haraniel. "Let's just calm down," I suggested, and my voice was strung tight as a harp string.

She swung her face toward me. Empty. There was nothing in her eyes. A cold shudder scrambled up my backbone. One step back bumped me into Haraniel, and I flinched at their hand on my shoulder.

An orderly ambled over and walked Roberta away before she could start screeching. Every drop of fear beaded on my skin. But Haraniel squeezed my shoulder, and warm courage spread from their fingertips.

"Let's go," they said. "There's been enough excitement today."

I tucked Mrs. van Horne's hand into the crook of my elbow. We followed behind Haraniel's exit. "You knew her name."

"I've talked with her mother. Horrible. She found Roberta in her bed, covered in dirt and . . . she was just as you see. Just like Mathilda."

"How long has she been here?"

"Since November," Mrs. van Horne said.

"November," I echoed. "Can you excuse me a moment?"

I stopped at the nursing station. The redhead behind the desk cocked a little smile at me. "Yes?"

"I wanted to ask about a patient. Roberta Howard. When was she admitted?"

A tiny wrinkle between her brows deepened and her lips pursed together. "Why do you want to know?"

"A hunch," I said. "Was it about November seventh?"

Her eyes flared open. I had her by the curiosity. "Yes. Why?"

I wasn't spilling that. Not without checking for proof. But I could have a list of all the Howards in Chicago as soon as I got my hands on a phonebook, and I'd bet every cent in my safe that her family lived close to a murder scene.

"It's probably nothing," I said. "Thanks."

Haraniel didn't say a word.

We took Mrs. van Horne to her Packard. She sat in the driver's seat, purse on her lap, her head bent as she fished inside the main compartment for her keys. The consent form for Mathilda's electroshock uncoiled, the top edge slightly bent, and I glanced away to give her grief a little room to breathe. What a horrible thing, to lose your child—but how much more horrible to still have her body, living, breathing, but empty of everything that made her yours, the girl you watched grow up?

Paper rustled. The gold-toned purse clasp clicked shut. Mrs. van Horne rolled down the window, offering her kid-gloved hand.

"Thank you," she said. "I don't know why you came to see Mathilda today, but—I'll tell the kitchen about the onions."

We stepped back as she started the engine and backed out of her spot, wheels jostling in snowy wheel ruts.

I dug my Chesterfields out of my pocket and lit up. Grackles landed on the snow and hopped closer, gathering around Haraniel's feet. Sparrows wheeled in the sky. I looked back at Dunning, reckoning which of the tall windows belonged to the common room.

All the pieces fit, tongue in groove, but I needed a smoke right now. It wouldn't make the truth go away. But I needed one more minute and the smoke to steady me.

I got twenty-two seconds before I made an angel fidget.

"What's our next lead?" Haraniel asked. "Do we interview the Howards?"

Birds hopped aside as I blew smoke into the breeze. "No. Next you tell me the truth."

Haraniel stood there with their mouth open. They licked their lips as their gaze slid away. "Whatever do you mean?"

"The birds, Haraniel. Mathilda's mother's dreams. The way those girls turned to you like a lodestone."

They dropped their chin, lashes lowered.

"I thought a demon had possessed Mathilda van Horne. But that's not true, is it?"

Haraniel turned her face away. "I hadn't told anyone. I didn't want it to be true. When Zashiel finds out, I don't know what they'll do . . . It can't be true. It can't."

"Say it, Haraniel."

They sighed. "You're right."

Not enough. "I'm right about what?"

"Those women were all hosts. Weak ones—enough power for a premonition and not much more. I think they were chosen precisely because they were weak, so the ordeal would break them." Haraniel looked back at me, thunder darkening Edith's eyes. "The White City Vampire is an angel, Elena. And that angel needs to be stopped."

4

WE HAD MILES to get back to the city and as much privacy as we could want, rolling past post-and-wire fences surrounding snowy fields, where some lay fallow for the winter and livestock wandered upon others. I settled my Chevy into the ruts on the road and took it easy going back.

"All right," I said around a freshly lit Chesterfield. "Tell me what's going on."

Haraniel folded their hands in front of them and mumbled at their knees.

"Speak up, angel."

"I said I should have told you. Edith's angry at me for holding back."

"How much does she know?"

"We both knew as soon as Edith saw those pictures you took. The script you didn't recognize? It's the human adaptation of angelic language. It's called Enochian."

I tore my eyes off the road to stare at them. "That's Enochian?"

Haraniel gripped the dashboard with both hands. "Please watch the road."

I steered back into my lane and waved at the guy speeding past and shaking his fist at me. "Enochian is the Brotherhood's biggest, closest secret. You have to be a third-degree initiate to study it."

That meant Ted knew about it, and didn't that thought worm in my brain? I pushed it aside and kept my eyes on the road.

"So, it's a language. Those sigils I didn't know—ideographs? Phonemes? An alphabet?"

"An alphabet. Enochian magic allows the initiate to communicate with and request aid of angels."

I huffed. "Seems to me you speak English pretty good."

"We hear all prayers, Elena. Most of them are demanding noise. Make this roll a seven. Get me the promotion at work. I want, I want, I want. One in a hundred thousand prayers are interesting enough to listen to, and those have trouble making it through. Enochian is a direct line to the Chorus."

"Okay, so, it's another old boys' network. That doesn't tell me why an angel is using women to kill the damned."

Haraniel bowed their head. They flinched as we hit a rut, teeth buried deep in Edith's lower lip.

"Oh, come on. You're afraid of cars?"

"My strength is greatly depleted after healing you and Edith. If you drive into something at this speed, our bodies will be hurt very badly."

"Believe me," I muttered. "I know."

"And you don't look at the road."

I huffed as I pointed my face toward the windshield. "We're fine. Listen. Marlowe hired me to find the White City Vampire because the victims all made deals. Somebody is getting in there and scooping up all her souls. What's the angel doing with them?"

We went half a mile before they opened their mouth. "Have you ever heard of the Grigori?"

"Sure. Angels sent to watch over humans on earth."

"We were the watchers, yes. The closest to the humans. Sometimes, an angel would come very close indeed."

I stole another glance at them. "You mean . . ."

Haraniel looked embarrassed. "It's not what you imagine. We thought so highly of our favored humans that we insinuated a piece of ourselves within their bodies. Their children were the Nephilim. They were born with magic and incredible creative potential, and they passed those gifts on to their children. Most of the lines are diluted now, but there are still strong descendants. Like Edith. Like you."

I went tense with surprise. The car obeyed my pressure on the gas pedal, engine roaring. Haraniel lurched over to grab at the wheel, but I batted their hand away.

"Stop that."

"This is dangerous."

"Keep your hair on. I've got it." I kept my eyes on the road. "Magicians and psychics are your umpty-ump great-grandchildren."

"What we did set Heaven in an uproar. We were ordered to abandon Earth and face punishment. Some went and were presumably forgiven. Others—*we* disobeyed."

"You said no to God? From what I hear, He doesn't like that much."

Haraniel's mouth flattened. They waggled their head, half-evasive but rueful. "We were the watchers. We were supposed to protect and guide you. If we left you alone . . . But the orders of Heaven mattered more than our sense of duty to you. And so, the way to Heaven closed."

Farms gave way to houses on smaller lots. We were entering the borderland, that belt of property that wasn't quite city and wasn't quite farm. "And now you're trapped down here. And you want to go back?"

Haraniel let their head fall back. They let out a gusty sigh. "We're tired, Elena. We're tired and we're weak. Once, I could destroy walled cities, devastate armies, translocate wherever I pleased. Now I can't even call your soul back to your body if you die. I'm a shell of what I once was."

I spotted a gas station and pulled in, giving the boy at the pump two dollars to fill the tank. Haraniel huddled in their seat, staring at their folded hands. I let them stew. Honestly, I needed the time to think. There was a lot more to the story; I knew that.

But they were dancing around the question I had asked, over and over again.

I waited until we were back on the road. "You still haven't told me why an angel would need a damned soul."

"Because I don't want to think about it."

"That bad?" I glanced at them. "What good are they to you? Hell, why do demons want them?"

"They're priceless. With the power of your soul in my hands—I could do things I haven't been able to do in centuries."

"So, whatever the angel is trying to do is so powerful that it takes an entire soul to power it—No. More than one soul, isn't it? Is that because they need more than one try, or because they need that much power to juice their operation?"

"I don't know."

"Don't give me that. What does an angel need that much power for? What's big enough to do anything for?"

Haraniel shook their head, but I guessed. You don't do the unthinkable to get something you want. You do it to get back what you lost.

Chicago spread out in front of us, and we rode right over the threshold. "They want to go home. They're trying to open the way to Heaven."

"I think so. Yes."

"But why *these* souls?"

"Elena," Haraniel said. "Isn't the answer obvious?"

I cast my attention back to the grim, stark road. I hadn't needed to ask the question. This way, an angel wouldn't be denying the fate of the righteous or harming a soul that had the potential to find their way back to the privilege of Heaven. The damned had forfeited that. By an angel's reckoning, we wouldn't count as victims.

I came to a stop sign. A group of rosy-cheeked children tumbled into the street, shepherded by their mother. My stomach shuddered as the sigils and geometry written in blood on the snow rose in my memory. "The markings were for a summoning?"

Haraniel's voice barely rose over the noise of the engine. "Yes."

"What—who is the angel summoning?"

"The most powerful of us," Haraniel said. "If anyone can open the way to Heaven, it's the archangel Michael. The square on the wall and on the last victim's chest was their name."

5

THAT PRONOUNCEMENT SHUT my mouth as we melded into Chicago traffic. I was one car in a school of drivers headed to Sunday dinners and evenings with families. One realization trickled in, and I cranked my window open for a faceful of January air.

"Marlowe said that I would be next," I said. "She said it was incentive. But I wasn't. You were there, and whoever is trying to summon Michael didn't want to tangle with you."

"We have to move quickly. Perhaps the killer doesn't know that we know. I have to tell Zashiel."

"And I have to talk to Marlowe. If she tells me whose tickets are coming up, it'll up our chances."

Haraniel pursed their lips. "I don't think we should split up. You're safe in the Reliance Building; those wards you cast are layered quite competently."

"Thank you."

If they heard my tone, they sure didn't act like it. "However, contacting your Marlowe is a problem. I can't get anywhere near a demon. I don't think I could control myself."

"There's another problem," I said. "I've been running full tilt since three in the morning. I need food. And rest."

"We can't spare the time. You can't spare the time."

I parked and cut the engine. "I'm no good to you if I pass out from hunger."

Haraniel grimaced, but they opened the passenger side and ambled over the snow-cleared sidewalk toward Joe's. I reached inside my handbag, found the plain gold band I always kept there, and put it on my finger.

"Hey. Edith's ring. Put it on."

Haraniel rolled their eyes, but they slipped the ring on their finger. They held the door for me, and steamy air redolent of fryer oil warmed my cheeks. The long counter and its round stools stood in an empty line, and green vinyl booths lined the wall of windows next to the sidewalk. "Moonlight Serenade" played from the jukebox. Our usual booth was empty, and copies of the *Tribune* lay next to the cash register.

"Where's Dorothy?" I called, and the waitress at the end of the long diner waved us to our booth. We crossed the green and black linoleum, shedding our coats as Dorothy came to fill white stoneware cups with coffee, leaving a little room in Edith's.

"Special is pot roast and braised vegetables with mash. Apple pie for dessert." Dorothy's voice was dulcimer-sweet. The coffee swayed inside the round glass carafe as she set it down.

"I love the pot roast," I said. "Edith?"

"Same," Haraniel answered, and then after a beat remembered to smile. "Thank you."

Dorothy bent over and pushed Haraniel's shoulder. "What's eating you, Edie?"

Haraniel shook their head. "Just glum, I guess."

"I made her miss *Inner Sanctum Mysteries* on the radio," I said, stepping in front of Dorothy's interrogation. "She's helping me with a research project."

"Oh, it was a good one tonight." Dorothy nodded, her eyes round as she pulled the order slip from her pad. "Chilled my blood! I'm sorry you missed it."

"I'll ask my boss to let me read the script at work tomorrow." Haraniel delivered those lines through a put-on smile, which made Dorothy tilt her head. Dorothy knew Edith, and Haraniel wasn't a convincing Edith.

I had to step in. "I suppose the game's on?"

"Radio's going in the kitchen. Do you want to hear it?"

"Just the score." I smiled at her over my cup. "Thanks, hon."

She walked away. I slumped for a relieved second and gave Haraniel the eye. "That was close. Maybe we should have gone somewhere else."

Somewhere the staff didn't know us, where they might not cook the pot roast with a little beer in it, but no one would blow the careful story of the sound engineer and the research assistant who met every Sunday to catch up now that our marriages had moved us apart. Haraniel shrugged and picked up the coffee cup. They sipped it black and their eyes widened. They set the cup down, mouth twisted in distaste.

"Ugh."

"Edith likes it with sugar and cream."

"That was . . . Why do you drink that? Don't answer."

Haraniel closed their eyes, and Edith opened them. Edith smiled at me, one corner tilted just a little higher than the other. A warm firework blossomed in my chest, the brilliant sparks flying along my nerves. I barely stopped myself from reaching across the table for her hand.

"Hi."

"Hi," Edith said.

She reached for the cream and sugar, doctoring her cup the way she liked it. Oh, my Edith. She touched the toes of our shoes together, and I couldn't smile at her like this. Somebody would see.

Silence followed the end of "Moonlight Serenade." Edith stirred sugar into her cup. "I need a nickel."

"I've got one."

Our fingers touched as I slid it across the tabletop. I rubbed the tips with my thumb. Edith plugged the nickel in the console at our table and flipped the pages. She would choose Billie Holiday and Tommy Dorsey, let them sing the words she couldn't say while we hung around there and talked fashion and work and our cover-story lives.

"Game's one-all," Dorothy said, and plates of slow cooked beef slid into place before us.

"That was fast."

"You two always buy the Sunday Special. Everything okay here?"

"Great," I said.

Dorothy bustled off. Edith hummed along as Frank Sinatra sang "Say It (Over and Over Again)" and I snuck another smile at her as she put her elbows on the table and went to work.

We didn't talk much, concentrating on refueling bodies deprived of food and rest. I could sleep for a hundred years. I'd be lucky if I got three hours.

Finally, Edith leaned back and sighed, draining her coffee cup. She eyed the last bit of pie crust on my plate, her eyebrows a high, worried arc. "Are you all right?"

"I should be asking you that."

She shrugged. "I'm fine. Tired."

"You should sleep."

She glanced around before leaning closer. "We should sleep."

We didn't stay to chat, leaving cash on the table plus two bits for a tip. The car was fine where it was, so we left it and took State Street up to the Reliance Building. We moved through the dim, warded lobby and into the elevator, and at last, Edith's fingers curled around mine.

"I should have told you."

"It was a secret, wasn't it?"

She leaned into my shoulder. "Are we supposed to have secrets?"

"Why shouldn't you? I have one."

She reached up to cup my cheek, her thumb sliding across my skin. "You never have to tell me, Helen. It won't change anything."

She'd be right, if I figured out how to trap an angel and get my soul back. I'd never have to tell her. But I wanted to when this was over. I wanted to purge it from my soul the minute I got it back. I would explain everything, and she would know how to listen, and love me anyway.

"But this is too big to keep to yourself, isn't it? I didn't know how to explain—"

"Listen. You are exactly who you were before I knew about Haraniel, got it? Even if they know how we—"

I bit my tongue. Edith smiled at me, and she led the way once the doors opened.

"I think we have time for that."

I followed her across the hallway, footsteps quickening as we dashed to my office.

6

I COULDN'T FIND a scar or a bump anywhere as I touched Edith in the dark. Not there, or there, or—

Her chest shook with her laugh. "What are you doing?"

"You got shot in the park." I didn't stop running my fingers over her skin, just for the silken pleasure of it.

She reached up and touched my shoulder. "So were you. Did it hurt?"

"Yes, but it didn't quite feel real. Did you hurt?"

"Only in the abstract. Haraniel took care of it." She sighed, and her fingertips grazed along my jaw. "I should have told you. Haraniel and I have been part of each other for a long time."

"How did you two become part of each other?"

"I prayed, and they answered. I was a child when Haraniel first came to me. They watched over me for years. Just a thought away. I understood what they were eventually and what they hoped I would do for them. And I did. I offered to be their host."

I propped myself up on one elbow so I could see the soft glow of the city kissing her cheek. "So, they're in you?"

"The angels exiled down here believe that if they bond with a host and live a human life, they will ascend to Heaven the moment their host dies."

"Is that so?"

Edith turned on her side, facing me as she tangled our legs together. "Well, no one knows. You have to take it on faith."

"Sounds awfully familiar," I said. "But the White City Vampire isn't so faithful."

"From what I understand, it's a lot to ask. The exiled are unused to humility, and to live a human life—to give up their autonomy—is the ultimate exercise in just that. But when I saw that photograph, when *we* saw it, that was too much."

"So, Haraniel, strictly speaking, shouldn't be on duty."

"Right," Edith said. "Haraniel really shouldn't be so involved, but they put the pieces together and they're . . . *Repulsed* isn't a strong-enough word. What this rogue angel is doing is abominable. They must be stopped."

I lowered my head and pulled her close. "I never wanted to pull you into this mess. All I ever wanted was to keep you safe . . . and it turns out you're a warrior."

"Haraniel's the warrior," Edith said. "They're usually content to abide within me, but this is too important. Once this is over, they'll settle back down. Lie back; you need to sleep."

She curled around me and was out a minute later. I needed sleep so badly, but I stared at the frost skating up the corner windows, the crystalline paths curving around the painted wards. We were safe. Warm, thanks to the radiator ticking in the corner. I pushed my nose into Edith's hair and breathed her in, closed my eyes, and let my bones rest.

I tried to fall trusting into sleep, but my nerves jangled at the downward slide away from consciousness. Sleep was too much like the oblivion of translocation. I couldn't let go, and maybe I would never welcome the arms of Morpheus again.

It took a long time before I lost the battle and slipped down into the dark.

And then I was awake, one bare foot on the rag rug and the other on the cool floor, my gun already in my hand. Something in the wards had set them quivering. The air was too thin. Vulnerable. I stepped over the boards and crouched, keeping low as

I crept halfway across the parlor toward the office. The hall lights glowed through the frosted glass of my front door, lettered with BRANDT INVESTIGATIONS—PLEASE WALK IN.

Someone had. A shadow sat before my desk, dark and tall, with a wide-brimmed hat pulled low. The shadow leaned on his elbow, fingers tapping on the arm of his chair.

I lowered the gun. I let out a sigh, and when I hit the light switch, I squinted at my brother, Ted.

ACT V

1

HE SAT THERE grinning as if he'd done something impressive, and he had. He'd gotten in there without tripping any of the alarms that should have gone off if a magician walked through the building's front doors, or managed to ride the elevator, or set shoe leather on the Italian marble floor before the booby-trapped door to my office. Hell, he'd probably thought dismantling all my wards was fun.

I stood there in my slip, arms akimbo just the way our mother used to stand on the top step and watch us gallop home while there was still a sliver of sun in the sky, and Ted's grin turned sheepish. His shoulders came up. But I didn't stop staring him down until he shifted in his seat, fidgeting. I kept my lips still while my head came up a little higher and the years between us disappeared.

"Sorry, Hells. I had to talk to you."

"My telephone works."

He shrugged, a trickle of winsome back in his smile. "You took your sweet time getting out of bed."

"I would have been dressed and waiting if you hadn't broken my wards. Rude, brother."

"So was the little curse you built into your wards to tag Brothers of the Compass," he shot back. "Aren't you going to ask me why I'm here?"

"No, because I know what you're going to say," I said. "'*Stay out of it, Hells. It's too dangerous. You don't know what you're dealing with.*' How am I doing so far?"

Ted laced his fingers together and laid them over his stomach. He tipped the chair back, teetering on its hind legs. "All right. How's this? I've got a plan. I can't let you screw it up. Just give me a day. One day, and then I'm all yours."

"My ticket's up tomorrow. If it isn't tomorrow already."

"Barricade yourself in here and sit tight. I'll take care of it."

"Oh, sure. You run off and work your plan while I read some Kipling and wait to die."

"You have to trust me."

"I have to save my own skin," I said. "There's an angel out there murdering people."

His eyes widened just a smidge before he put his smile back on, that *please sis* smile that won me over every time. "It's more complicated than that."

"So complicated my dainty little female brain can't grasp it?"

"Come on, Hells. Will you leave it be for one day?"

"Because you broke in here and said so? You really think I'm going to stand back, with everything that's on the line? It's my soul."

"You shouldn't have dealt it in the first place."

I sighed. "I don't want to have this fight. Pass me those matches?"

Ted stared at the bright little box on the desk. It twitched into the air, floating across the room to land neatly in my hand. I grabbed a half-crumpled pack and shook out a Chesterfield, busying myself with the match strike and the flare of light as I puffed a smoke into life. "You can still do that."

Ted shrugged. "I imagine you still get visions when you touch things."

"Not anymore. Would have come in handy on missing-persons cases. Now tell me how you're going to rescue me from the torment of Hell and why I should let you look the other way while an angel sacrifices souls."

His lips curled in. "How much do you know?"

"Enough to make a good guess." I dragged on my cigarette.

"The Brothers of the Compass have been buddies with exiled angels for ages. But your feathered friends lost the juice they had in the good old days. They want to get back upstairs before their power diminishes completely, and when they make it, their gratitude will mean more power for the Brotherhood."

Ted licked his lips. "I can intervene for you. I can't get you back in the Brotherhood, but I can save your soul. You gave everything to save me."

"And that's how you live with what this angel is doing," I said. "Those souls consumed, this soul saved. It's all right to ignore that damnation to save me from mine? What about Nightingale McIntyre and all the rest?"

"They didn't sacrifice their souls for love," Ted shook his head. "They wanted money. Fame. Attention. You gave your salvation for me."

"And they were damned anyway, right?" I closed my eyes. I gathered strength. "But what about the husked-out hosts the White City Vampire used to do those murders? What about all the innocents left to rot up in Dunning?"

He blinked at me. "What?"

His blank look throbbed in my temples. "You didn't know what happened to the hosts," I said. "That night with the blood-pointer spell, when the trail stopped in the street—that was where the angel dropped Mathilda van Horne like a pair of dirty socks."

Ted's shoulders came up. He ducked his chin. "I assumed the host was hit by a car. I put a researcher on it."

"They kept that from you, I guess. I can't see you going along with it otherwise. Your angel uses women—girls, really. They have Nephilim bloodlines, but they're not strong enough to handle what happens to them. Your killer uses them up and throws them away."

He stared in my direction as his good intentions came crashing down on him. I stood there in the silence, heat from the radiator warming one flank, the soft crackle of burning tobacco swelling as I took another drag.

A prickle scurried up the back of my neck. Danger. Where? What?

A hum, dull and dangerous. The elevator of an otherwise empty office building, climbing up to the fourteenth floor.

My gun came up. Ted's did too. But we didn't fire as the door swung open and Delaney stood in the frame, his own ugly little automatic pointed straight at me.

Ted put his gun down. "Delaney. You don't need that."

"She needs a hole put in her."

"Don't talk about my sister that way." Teddy stood up and moved left, putting himself between me and Delaney's bean-shooter. "You don't need to do this. She'll stay out of it."

"That's what you're going to do with your bargain? You're going to save your warlock sister?"

"I know the Perfect said she was the only vessel strong enough. But you can't use her for the last manifestation."

My throat went dry. An angel needed a body descended from the Nephilim. And they couldn't grab any old psychic to do the job. They needed someone with more power.

The White City Vampire had skipped me as a victim because they wanted my body for a host.

And Ted—my sweet, idiot brother Ted—had waltzed right into my stronghold and taken down all my wards. He had wanted to keep me safe, but instead he'd cracked open Fort Knox for them, thinking he could handle everything himself.

"You're right," Delaney said. "We can't use her for the last manifestation. She's tainted. She would never make a worthy vessel for the first sword of the army of God."

In the fluorescent light from the hall, Delaney's eyes shone like silver mirrors. Like they'd shone in the photo I'd snapped of him and Ted in the alley. Like all those failed pictures of Edith.

Oh, no.

Ted's shoulders slid down an inch. I lifted my gun and spread my feet, sighting down the top, my heart pounding. "Ted—"

The door from the parlor creaked as Edith swung it open, unarmed and in her slip.

Get down! I tried to shout. But Edith barreled across the room, charging straight for Delaney. My heart was in my throat: Edith, the most pure, the most worthy woman, previously protected by my wards; of course they hadn't come for me but for *her*—

Except Delaney dodged Edith. He dove for Ted and seized his wrist.

"It's you, Magus Brandt. You're the worthy one," he said, and light flared around them both an instant before Delaney and my brother vanished.

2

GONE. NOTHING LEFT but a smudge in the air where they used to be, the shape of my brother and the angel who took him stamped on my sight like a negative. I stared at it, trying to rebuild what was once there through will alone, something clutching around my heart as a scream trembled in my throat. Gone. Gone, taken, kidnapped—because he was the worthy vessel that my soulless body was not.

This was my fault.

Edith's hands clenched around my biceps. "Elena!"

I jostled, the afterimage of brother and angel shaking as the last shred of their presence melted into nothing. Gone, and I stared at Haraniel squinting at me through Edith's eyes.

"Elena." Haraniel's grip on my arms fell away. A sharp snap next to my right ear, my left. "Elena. Here and now. What happened to the wards?"

I let go of the breath I'd strangled to keep from screaming. "Where'd they go?"

"I don't know." Haraniel dragged me back to the room where my bed rested. They started flinging clothes at me. "The wards, Elena. What happened? We were protected."

I hopped around on one foot, yanked my trousers up to my waist, and caught a brassiere in mid-flight. "Ted got cute and broke them all when he busted in to talk to me."

Haraniel misbuttoned Edith's blouse as they let out a string of harsh syllables. I didn't need to know the tongue to see the air turn blue. "We need help, fast. Zashiel can call everybody in."

I tied my shoes over bare feet, lurched across the room to pick up my revolver, and caught my overcoat and hat after Haraniel summoned them to their hands.

"We must make haste," Haraniel urged.

I slipped my fingers into my pocket, and smooth, enchanted silk met my skin. I kept my gun in hand and nodded, even though I was screaming inside at facing the void again. *Never mind that. They've got my brother.* "Let's hit the road."

We shattered into six billion pieces and came together in the nave of Saint Stanislaus. The saints staring down at us didn't unnerve me this time, but I looked hard at the one who stood in pride of place—Michael the archangel, sword in his hand.

It made something cold trickle down my neck. "Haraniel—"

But they were already running full tilt for the sacristy. I dashed after them, but they were fast as Atalanta, down the stairs before I could stop them. I leapt over the last half of the flight, trying to close the distance. *Haraniel. Haraniel, stop. Wait.*

They skidded to a stop before an iron-banded door. I galloped through the reek of frankincense, choked on it as I drew in breath to shout. *Stop. Stop!*

The angel in Edith's body flung the door open and rushed inside. "Zashiel! Something terrible has—"

Too late, I caught up to them, laid a quelling hand on their shoulder. Too late.

We were in a big room fit for a catechism class, if it were not every inch of it painted in blood. Symbols covered every surface—so many, I couldn't decipher them all if I had a month, and we didn't have a minute.

I knew the gist. They spread all over the floor and up the walls, every line prepared by the same hand. Protection. Supplication. Summoning.

And kneeling, naked, and shackled to the floor—that was Ted, struggling with all his might to get free. Zashiel stood over him and poured clear liquid on his head, chanting in Latin: *Purge me with hyssop, and I will be clean; wash me, and I will be whiter than snow.*

The ritual had begun.

Haraniel reached inside their coat and drew out a dagger, all silver and shining, the blade etched in Enochian glyphs. They raised the blade before them and it lengthened into a sword, emanating a power that pressed on my skin. Edith's body was taller, stamped in light and righteous might, and my stomach shivered in awe and dread as the shadow of Haraniel's wings fell over Ted's shoulders.

"Zashiel," they said. "Stop this. Repent of it."

From where I stood, I could see how their hands shook.

Zashiel looked up for half an instant and pursed their lips. "Haraniel. It's finally over. It's time for us to go home."

Their fingers tightened in Teddy's wet hair. They shook my brother like a puppy, but Ted kept trying to free his wrists from the shackles regardless. I fought the soul-deep urge to run to him, to leap at Zashiel, knock them flat, and beat their head against the glyph-covered floor until they stopped moving. My need for violence flashed over my scalp like red lightning.

I stayed still and quiet and waiting, my fingers tucked into the opposite cuff of my coat.

Haraniel raised the sword a little higher. "Brother. Please. If you do this, Theodore will die."

Zashiel shrugged, their mouth stretched in a dismissive line. "He was snatched from his destined rest years ago. He's longed for Heaven ever since."

I cast a worried glance at Ted. Was that true? Did he want—

Ted tried to tuck his thumb to pull his hand clear again. I saw his joint strain close to breaking. Haraniel took a step closer, and

Zashiel tracked them a little more intently now. "Do you think you have a place in Heaven with the stain of murder on your hands? This is monstrous."

Yes. Yes, keep talking. I stared hard at Ted, willing him to look up from his struggle, to look at me, thinking at him as hard as I could. *Ted. Teddy. Ted, look at me. Look—*

He raised his chin and looked me in the eye.

"I do what I must," Zashiel said. "Every day diminishes us further. Every day drags us down into this clay—We stand on the brink, Haraniel! Don't you see what will become of us if we don't restore ourselves now?"

"There is a way back for all of us," Haraniel said. "You know the way. To live in humility, joined with our host in a mortal life. To live a life dedicated to their good work, to face a mortal death with them so they might deliver us to Heaven, where we can repent—"

"All those angels, dead and gone, every one of them promising to send the rest of us a sign." Zashiel shook their head, gentle with pity for Haraniel. "All those angels, and not a single one has ever, ever sent the sign they promised. Not for centuries. No matter how hard or how far or how deep we have searched—there is not one sign from any of them."

The tip of Haraniel's sword dipped half an inch. Edith's angel looked upon their leader, dismay in every line of their face.

"Zashiel, you have fallen," they said, and the words quivered in the still air. "My friend, oh, my friend. You have lost your faith."

Zashiel flinched, and their mouth thinned as rage rammed their spine bolt upright.

Hells.

Teddy's voice in my head, clear as a bell. I slipped my hand out of my coat cuff and threw the lockpick in a smooth underhand lob. It landed short and to the left of Teddy's knee with an audible *plink.*

Shit.

Haraniel turned their head, tracking the noise. Zashiel made a sign with their fingers, twisted them into another, and pushed the air.

Haraniel's sword clattered to the floor. They hit the wall, their head connecting with a thump. They grabbed at their throat, their mouth open and eyes wide.

Zashiel sneered. "I've endured this interruption long enough."

Shit. There was only one thing left to do, and I was the only damn fool in the room left to do it. I stepped in front of Haraniel. I pulled my revolver out of my coat and leveled it at Zashiel.

"Let Haraniel go," I said, and my voice didn't waver at all. "Let them both go."

They tutted their tongue. "Elena, you know the Chaldean hours as well as I do. The time is right. I can't stop now."

No time for smart-mouthed banter. I squeezed the trigger.

A hole bored into Zashiel's surplice and cassock, a scarlet flower blooming just over their heart. They staggered, letting go of my brother's hair to windmill their arms against falling.

Behind me, Haraniel collapsed to the floor, their gasping breaths like music. "Helen. Zashiel did something. I can't . . ."

Haraniel never called me Helen. That was Edith. My breath caught. We were down our heavy hitter, and it all rode on me.

Zashiel regained their balance and glared so hard at me, my guts turned to water. "Monkey, that *hurt.*"

I shot them again for want of a snappy comeback.

It rocked them back a step, but they were braced this time. They put on an ugly face and marched toward me. One step. Two.

I sighted down my revolver and put another enchanted bullet in their lung. Something in these bullets was hurting them. Maybe I'd live to figure out what it was.

They staggered, and blood sprayed from their mouth as they coughed. Still standing. I adjusted my aim and drilled one right in the middle of their forehead. *Fall, you bastard. Fall down and stay down.*

They kept coming even as two more tore up their face. I was out of bullets and bright ideas. I took a swing at them, but they gave me a tap to the belly that had me wheezing for breath. They took the revolver from my hand and whipped it across my face.

A tooth wiggled. Blood poured over my tongue. I landed on my knees and fumbled the handkerchief out of my pocket. I wiped my mouth with it, bright drops sinking into the painted silk. "Uncle."

Zashiel smirked. Bullets oozed out of their wounds. The wounds closed, smoothed over, and were left whole. "Do you really think you can ask for mercy, soulless? Do you honestly believe I will grant it?"

Teddy had quit thrashing around. I looked up at Zashiel, their shadow falling over my face. "Let my brother go. Use me."

They hit me with my own gun again. I landed on the glyph-covered floor and they stood over me, smirking.

"You think I'd settle for you when I have him? Every bit as powerful as you but pure. Unsullied. More fitting for my eldest brother."

I covered my mouth with the handkerchief. I muttered into its silken folds and tried to press my tooth back into its socket.

Zashiel cocked his head, dark button eyes shining. "What was that?"

"Sorry." I grinned at him with bloody teeth. "I said, *O diabole, venī auxiliō meō*!"

I unfurled the handkerchief and held it on display, showing him the summoning circle, painted on silk and charged with my own blood.

A stink like burnt matches and rotten eggs fought with the opoponax-and-jasmine scent of Shalimar, and there stood Marlowe, a gray fedora over her platinum curls. A pinstripe double-breasted suit hung bespoke on her shoulders, her smiling lips shiny and red as blood.

"Hello, darling. Found my soul-thief, have you?"

"He's all yours," I said. "My soul?"

"As agreed."

Marlowe snapped her fingers and the sound settled in my chest. It quivered like a struck gong, my soul returned to its home. It spread inside me with the prickle of snowflakes on skin, reaching through every nerve and muscle and bone. My soul was home, and I was whole.

I breathed a little deeper. "Thanks, doll."

"It was my pleasure. You might not want to watch this," Marlowe said. "I don't believe in quick deaths. It could get ugly in here—"

Movement just at the edge of my vision was all the warning I had before Delaney busted through the chamber doors and jumped her.

They went down in a vicious, punching heap. Marlowe's fedora tumbled to the floor, only to be crushed by the grappling pair. Marlowe buried one crimson-lacquered thumbnail in Delaney's left eye. It was all he deserved, but I couldn't stand there and watch like I had ringside seats.

I dove for Edith, who blinked at me as she felt the back of her head. She spared half a second to register who I was before her gaze flicked over my shoulder.

Aw, shit. That's right. I had a dance booked with an angel who had no reason to love me, after I'd shot up their face and all. I spun to face the hate in their eyes.

"You little weasel," they said. Another of those long, silvery daggers manifested in their hand, and as I watched the thing that was probably going to kill me, I wondered if it was made from the iron of a dead star.

Edith nudged my hand, and my fingers wrapped around the barrel of the gun I'd cajoled her into carrying. It wouldn't kill him. It would buy us a few seconds at most. Good enough. I didn't need to beat an angel. I just needed them distracted. I put enchanted iron in Zashiel as fast as I could cock the hammer and squeeze. They rocked a little. Blood trickled down the side of their nose as they rushed me.

I dropped my aim and took them in the knee. That made them stumble, and as they bent to watch the bullet expel and the flesh knit itself back up, I took four more chances to make Swiss cheese of their head.

That just reminded them I was there. They closed the distance, unstoppable, unkillable, and I wondered if I would go to Heaven as they dropped their arm a little to come in low.

Something knocked into my hip and I went down. Pain jolted from the heel of my hand to my elbow just before I hit the floor. My wrist throbbed hot—something in there had busted—and I looked back.

Edith stood in my place.

Zashiel stabbed, street-fight perfect. The point drove into her solar plexus, the angle tilted up. Edith, her eyes and mouth wide, a soft hiss of air escaping instead of a scream.

No. Oh, no, no . . .

Zashiel pulled the blade out, and Edith bent forward. Blood spilled, falling on summoning glyphs.

I was on my feet, finally. Too late. Too late. Edith turned her head to look at me, her summer-sky eyes focused on my face. I reached her just in time to see the light in those eyes go out. I grabbed for her as every joint unlocked and she fell to the ground.

No. Please. Edith . . .

Zashiel snarled and swung for me, their knife covered in Edith's blood.

My life wasn't worth anything, but I fought for it just the same. I caught their wrist and dug my fingers in a sensitive point; they kept their grip on the knife and tore their hand away. They came at me again, the blade low and swinging fast, but I'd played my hand when I tried to disarm them. It was done.

Zashiel looked me in the eye, teeth bared—and then light poured from their eyes, their nose, their open, silent mouth. They arched like a pulled bow as the light bled out of them, leaving the afterimage of their surprise as they fell beside Edith.

Ted stood over them, Haraniel's blade in his hand. He looked down at Zashiel's body, breathing hard.

Fuck, no. Not Teddy. Not this. I fought the burr in my throat, fought the tears burning my eyes and nose. "Ted."

What have you done, I wanted to say. *What have you done to your soul this day, oh Ted, oh little brother—*

"Helen. Helen! Are you all right?"

Nothing would ever be right again. Edith's blue, blue eyes stared at nothing, and I was nothing, nothing without her.

Light flooded the room for two heartbeats. Another body thumped to the floor. Marlowe pushed herself to her feet and pulled out a handkerchief to dab at a drop of blood that had landed on her cheek. She gave Delaney's body an angry glare and stepped over it, blood spattered all over her pinstripe suit.

"What a mess," she muttered. "All right, love?"

I didn't answer. I turned and kneeled next to Edith. I gathered her into my arms. She was heavy, her limbs loose and awkward. I clasped her to my chest, and I could still smell her perfume.

Once upon a time, I had walked into a secret queer bar, and the woman who would be the love of my life asked me to dance. She hadn't known whether to lead or to follow, but she put her hand on my waist and did her best as she stepped all over my toes. Later that night, as we walked under a diamond-studded sky up the shore of Lake Michigan, she made up for not knowing how to dance by kissing me so sweet, the earth stood still to watch it.

I never told her how she had saved me. I never told her how she became the dearest friend I'd ever had. I told her I loved her, but never enough. My Edith of the sparrows. My heart. My world.

I wasn't all right.

But I could be.

I looked up. "Marlowe. Marlowe, she's dead."

Marlowe stepped closer, moving slow. She stood over the two

of us, looking down at me, at dead, gone Edith in my arms. There was nothing on her face as she gazed at the two of us, and then, so smooth I nearly heard the click, her expression bloomed into sympathy.

"Helen. Dear Helen. I'm so sorry, darling." She crouched next to me and smoothed one of Edith's curls. "Let's close her eyes, now."

"No." I squeezed Edith tight. "Bring her back."

Teddy's mouth fell open. "What?"

But Marlowe didn't look surprised at all. She tilted her pretty head, and she lifted a lock of hair out of my eyes, so gentle it almost shattered me. "Are you sure?"

"Bring her back."

"Helen," Teddy said, but we neither of us listened to him.

"What I did for you, Helen, no devil does that. No one ever earned their way out of a deal before. And no one ever will again."

"Helen. Don't do this. She's in Heaven. You'll go there too," Teddy said.

"But you won't," I said.

I didn't want to live without Edith. I couldn't leave Ted lonely down in Hell.

This seemed best. "Marlowe."

She gazed at me and Edith a little longer.

I lifted my head and swiped at my cheeks. "Marlowe. Please."

She stood there, thinking. Deciding. Then I saw it shift into place just behind her eyes.

"Why, this is Hell, nor am I out of it," Marlowe murmured. She gave me a wistful smile. "Ah, love. My usual terms. Ten years."

"Good enough. Do it."

Marlowe knelt in blood, caught my chin, and gave me a gentle, lingering kiss.

In my arms, Edith gasped for breath.

3

EDITH. EDITH BREATHING, gazing up at me through June-sky eyes, whole and alive and there. I pressed my forehead to hers and washed the blood off her face with my tears. Edith was alive and I was something once more.

But she wiggled in my embrace, trying to sit up on her own. She held her hands up before her face, flexing her fingers in the practiced motions of a pianist limbering her joints. She let out a quivering breath and raised her face to mine.

"I was dead."

Behind me, Ted made a strangled, despair-soaked noise.

I bent my head and looked at her knee, poking through a rent in her trousers, and waited for her next words to fall on my neck.

"We were in Heaven. Haraniel and I. We were there," Edith said, and Ted's face flashed up in my memories, pale and cold and horrified, his lips curling around the same words ten years ago. "Helen. How . . ."

I owed her the sight of my eyes at least. I looked up, ready for disgust, and gave her a ten-year-old reason, the only one I ever had—

"I would do anything for you. And I did."

She went still and staring and so, so quiet. Not a single breath sighed in that room as she watched me, her brow furrowed, her mouth open, her thoughts dashing madly in the back of her gaze as she realized what I must have done.

And then she exhaled, tears welling in her eyes. "Oh, Helen. My darling. My lonely soul."

She reached up and fit my cheek into the soft curve of her hand. Someone sobbed, and I was curled up in Edith's arms, my face in her neck, and she kept me safe as I shuddered and let everything fall apart.

She kissed my hair. She stroked my back. And behind me, Teddy wept in heart-torn mourning.

Her warm hand lifted off my back, and an awkward giant crashed into us. Teddy's long arms looped around me as he cried like the child who'd lost everyone in a single skidding instant. We twisted around and held him tight, and if Edith cared one bit that her introduction to my brother came when he was stark naked and bawling his eyes out, she didn't show it. My Edith, my beloved, with her heart as big as the world.

But Ted collected himself eventually, sniffing and hitching. "You did it again. You just—I just got you back, and you—"

He remembered he was in his birthday suit, from the way he glanced at Edith with red cheeks. He let his hands cover over his lap. Edith smiled at his blushing face and untangled herself from the clump, giving us a little distance.

He turned his head away, letting his expression run free for a few heartbeats before he turned back. "Why?"

"The world's no good without you, Ted. And it's no good without her."

"But you're damned again."

"And so are you. You whacked an angel, little brother. I hear they get sore about that upstairs."

"He was going to kill you. And then you—" He closed his eyes. "Is she worth it?"

I tipped up his chin with gentle fingers. "You saved my life. Was I worth it?"

He sighed, letting his shoulders fall. "I didn't really understand until it was your life on the line and I could do something about it."

"Oh, kid. They'll kick you out of the Brotherhood, you know."

"Yeah."

"I'm sorry."

"I don't care. You were going to die. I only just got you back. I—"

Oh, it hurt. It hurt to feel loved like this, to know that Ted had damned himself to save me. "I know a thing or two about being a warlock. It's only lonely sometimes."

"Could be." He tilted his head and waggled it in the way that means *It might be so, but it doesn't matter.* Then a smile crept up his mouth. "You need a partner in the private-eye business?"

I couldn't help my relieved laughter—the reflex of survival. "I think we're relocating out west."

"Ahem."

We looked up.

Marlowe and Edith stood a little ways off, and faintly, I heard the wail of police sirens. Marlowe moved closer and paused to look Teddy up and down with a slow, roaming eye. "Charming as you are in your birthday suit, Mr. Brandt, I think the gentlemen in blue are coming for a visit. It's time to scram. Join hands, now; come along—"

Ted held my left hand. Edith held my right. Marlowe caught my eye and winked just as the thunder of running boots trampled overhead. The matchstick scent of sulfur bloomed just before we joined with the void.

We materialized in Marlowe's rose-scented suite next to the windows that peered at Lake Michigan, right in the middle of her plush white rug. Julian appeared at the threshold like he'd been sitting up all night, waiting for the demon prince of Chicago to come home.

"Good evening, Miss Marlowe."

"Julian. I brought guests. Will you fetch Mr. Brandt a dressing gown, please?"

"Shall I call for Mr. Henry at Johnson and Sons, Miss?"

"First thing in the morning," Marlowe confirmed, and then eyed up my brother again. "What are you, handsome? About a forty-two long?"

He fidgeted only a little as he nodded. "A size thirteen shoe."

"We'll get you fixed up first thing in the morning," Marlowe promised. "Now, after a night like that, what a body needs is a nice long bath, and I know just the tub for you. Come on, step lively, don't worry about the rug . . ."

Marlowe led, and with one last frazzled glance at me, Teddy followed. Edith and I looked at each other with some bemusement until she turned serious.

"You sold your soul."

"I'd do it again in a minute."

"We'll have to bury you. Ted and I." Edith grabbed me by the lapels and dragged me in. "Ten years. That's all we have?"

"Don't you want it?"

"That's not the point! You—"

"It is for me. Ten years with you? You bet I want it. Every second."

She had tears in her eyes. "It's not enough."

"We'll make do." I touched her cheek. "Everything you want, baby. Anything you want. Name it and it's yours."

"I want the moon."

"I'll get a ladder."

She laughed, and it mended my heart. "You are going to regret promising me that."

I clutched her to me. "I never will."

4

WE LAY TOGETHER on a round silken bed on the city side of Marlowe's suite, and I had Edith's earlobe between my teeth. The moon peeped in our windows, but she was pretty good at keeping secrets. Edith sighed and snuggled into my neck, kissing in the hollow just above my collarbone.

"More?"

"In a minute," I said. "What happened to Haraniel?"

Her fingers drifted over my shoulder. "We died. We went to Heaven. I came back. They stayed home."

"So, you're alone now."

"In a way," Edith said. "We're still connected, even though Heaven's locked."

"So, you can talk to them? Can I send them a message?"

Edith chuckled. "You can if you like, but they're pretty sore at you. They think what you did was selfish."

"Well." I licked dry lips and looked away. "I guess that says it all."

"But I'm selfish too," Edith said. "I didn't want you to die on your birthday. Or at all."

I glanced back at her. "You knew?"

She tapped my temple. "You'd been thinking about it a lot lately."

I shook my head and kissed her just above the eyebrow. "I should have known I couldn't keep it secret from you, baby. Are you sore at me for yanking you out of Heaven?"

"Heaven can wait if I get ten more years with you."

Ten years. It wasn't enough time, but I would live every blessed second of it. "We're going to San Francisco."

She smiled up at me. "We'll get a house in North Beach."

"Right away," I said. "I've got the down payment and then some."

She sighed and pulled me close. "We're going to be so happy."

We would be. I'd dust the knickknacks, burn the sausage, wake up next to her every morning. I'd be grateful, even though I knew the end.

ACKNOWLEDGMENTS

As always, no story comes together without help. Dr. A. J. Townsend has read this story so many times, from its first incarnation to the final major revision. Elizabeth Bear read it when I regretted tucking it in a drawer, and her feedback prompted me to pull it out again and refashion the story some more, in search of the right home. Caitlin McDonald, my agent, helped to give it one last polish before sending this story out to seek its fortune, and that brought me back to working with Carl Engle-Laird, who kept the atmosphere and silver-screen-and-shadow feel of the story all silk.

Thanks to everyone at Tordotcom who did all the things that make a book shine. To Irene Gallo, publisher extraordinary, who kept this project on track and ticking. To Matt Rusin, editorial assistant, keeping all our ducks in a row a dozen times a week. For *ETIKTE*'s jacket designer, Christine Foltzer, who sent this book out dressed to kill, and to Mark Smith, the artist who reached right into the story and put its beating heart on the cover. To Becky Yeager and Michael Dudding, marketing marvels wearing out shoe leather while taking this book out on the town. To my production editor, Megan Kiddoo (again!), taking care of the i's, the t's, the p's, and the q's. To Jim Kapp, production manager, who kept everyone and everything headed toward getting the book on the shelves. To my publicist, Giselle Gonzalez, who arranged a bushel of events to get this story out to the readers. For my designer, Heather Saunders, who took care of the details that make the book easy on the eyes. For Richard Shealy, who, I am pleased to say, copy edited this book with care and attention. And to Angie Rao, who designed the promotional material and ads for the story. Y'all are great. Thanks heaps.